"Oh, what the devil!" His solemn face broke into an impish grin. *"Might as well be hanged for a sheep as a lamb."*

He pulled her tight against him, and though she quickly turned her head to avoid his lips, they found their target with practiced ease.

This time she thought she knew what to expect. She was not the least bit fooled by the meteor shower that fell around her. Her own senses, and not the heavens, were producing this phenomenon. It wasn't fair, some almost-drowned inner voice protested weakly. She had dreamed of this. Being clasped in strong male arms and kissed to the very edge of distraction and beyond, in just the way the novels she and Emmy had read beneath the bed covers at school had described it. But it was Sir Galahad that she had dreamed of. And here was Mordred turning her into an abandoned woman totally unlike herself.

Also by Marian Devon
Published by Fawcett Books:

MISS ARMSTEAD WEARS BLACK GLOVES
MISS ROMNEY FLIES TOO HIGH
M'LADY RIDES FOR A FALL
SCANDAL BROTH
SIR SHAM
A QUESTION OF CLASS
ESCAPADE
FORTUNES OF THE HEART
MISS OSBORNE MISBEHAVES
LADY HARRIET TAKES CHARGE
MISTLETOE AND FOLLY
A SEASON FOR SCANDAL

A HEART
ON HIS
SLEEVE

Marian Devon

FAWCETT CREST • NEW YORK

A Fawcett Crest Book
Published by Ballantine Books
Copyright © 1992 by Marian Pope Rettke

All rights reserved under International and Pan-American Copyright Conventions. Published in the United States by Ballantine Books, a division of Random House, Inc., New York, and simultaneously in Canada by Random House of Canada Limited, Toronto.

Library of Congress Catalog Card Number: 92-97060

ISBN: 0-449-22160-1

Manufactured in the United States of America

First Edition: February 1993

Chapter One

" '*To-morrow is Saint Valentine's day.*' "

Miss Emeline Sedley was gazing out the bow window of her bedchamber with a faraway look in her eyes.

"No, Emmy, you mistake the matter." Miss Andrea Prior, guest of Miss Sedley, did not bother to glance up from her tambouring hoop. She had had quite enough, thank you, of the February rain that seemed to hold such a fascination for her friend. "Valentine's Day is a full two weeks away."

Emmy turned impatiently from her kneeling position on the window seat. "I was quoting, peagoose. *Hamlet.* You, of all people, should know that. You're practically a bluestocking."

"I'm no such thing," Andrea denied emphatically. "And even if I were, how should you expect me to recognize a phrase like that? You might as

1

well have said 'I have seen nothing.' That's from *Hamlet*, too, but when one hears it the Bard doesn't instantly leap to mind. If you're trying to be literate, 'To be or not to be' would be more to the point."

"Oh, bother fusty old Hamlet! He has nothing to say in the matter. Valentine's Day is the point. And the only reason I brought up *Hamlet* is that I was thinking about the time when Miss Monkhouse's class read the play to the entire school and she chose me for Ophelia. Remember?"

"I'm not likely to forget." Andrea wrinkled her nose in distaste. "I was Hamlet."

"No need to take that tone. You should have been flattered. Yours was the leading role."

"Flattered? To be chosen for a man's part? You might recall that I wished to be Gertrude."

"Yes, but since men are as rare as unicorns in female academies, I think you can simply assume that the Monk considered you the best reader in the class."

"Oh, you think so?" Andrea refused to be mollified. "She *said* that I looked boyish."

Her friend giggled. "You should not have taken it so to heart. You'd just had a growing spurt and were taller than most of us, that's all. I can assure you, Andrea"—she gave the other an admiring look—"no one could possibly accuse you now of looking boyish. But I do wish you would not change the subject. For we have strayed ridiculously away from the point."

"Oh, I do beg pardon. I'd no notion that there was one. What is it?"

"What Ophelia said. You see, I never gave it any thought at the time. It seemed like so much gibberish. For the poor thing was supposed to have been

2

mad as a hatter, remember? But in this instance she knew precisely what she was talking about."

"That the next day was St. Valentine's? Well, actually, it wasn't."

"Oh, never mind the fusty old calendar. That's not the point either."

"Now, are you quite sure there is one?" Andrea picked up her scissors and snipped a thread.

"Yes, for it's Ophelia's entire speech that's important, not whether she got the date right. So will you please listen?" Emmy jumped down from the window seat to strike a theatrical attitude and declaim:

> "To-morrow is Saint Valentine's day,
>   All in the morning betime,
> And I a maid at your window,
>   To be your Valentine.

"Now do you understand?"

"Why, yes, I collect I do. The poor girl was clearly out of her mind, a raving bedlamite." Andrea smiled mischievously. "Only perhaps you should roll your eyes a bit more. Think of Edmund Kean playing Othello."

"Quit funning and listen." Emmy plopped down on the rose-decorated carpet at Andrea's feet. "Ophelia might have been mixed up on the date," she explained earnestly, "but she had the *custom* right. Did you know that it is an old, old, old belief that you'll marry the first man you see on St. Valentine's Day?" Her eyes were wide and solemn as she fastened them on her friend.

"What a ghastly thought. Remind me to stay in all of February fourteenth with my head underneath my pillow. I'd certainly not wish to see one of the gardeners or the butler or some tradesman up from the village and be leg-shackled to him for life."

"Oh, it wouldn't work like that." Emmy gave the thought a dismissive wave.

"Whyever not? Can you tell me who else is likely to come past our window?"

"The men we're going to marry! Pay attention, pray. That's the whole point, you lobcock!"

"Well, in the five days we've spent here since we came down from the academy, the types I've mentioned are the only ones of the masculine persuasion who have come near the dower house. Hardly husband material."

"But don't you see? That just goes to show how important Valentine's Day is. For here we are, fast approaching spinsterhood, with not a beau between us."

" 'Fast approaching spinsterhood'! Isn't that doing it up a bit too brown? Oh, I'll admit I'll soon be nineteen, but you're only just eighteen. Surely we don't have to don our caps quite yet. Besides, you needn't make staying single sound like a fate worse than death."

"Well, it is. And just look at us. Why, I should be making my come-out at this very minute and instead I'm stuck in this backwater for another year at least. And as for you—" She suddenly stopped her tirade and looked flustered.

"And as for me," her friend calmly finished for her, "I'll not be making a come-out at all."

"Of course you will!" Emmy's false heartiness belied the assurance. "Your father's bound to come about. But in the meantime . . ." She paused dramatically.

"Yes? In the meantime?"

"There's St. Valentine's Day. And I for one mean to use it for all it's worth."

Andrea looked amused. "And just what is it worth, Emmy? Tuppence?"

"Don't scoff. It's worth far more than you'd ever imagine. For I've been asking around, you see. And you'd be amazed at the things the old ones will tell you. Why, Grandmama herself is a regular font of information about ancient customs."

"Indeed?"

In all honesty Andrea could not imagine the formidable dowager ever having had an interest in Valentine's Day.

"Oh, yes, indeed. I've learned that there is no end of ways to discover your future. And I for one mean to explore them all. There are ways to dream about your valentine. And other ways to actually see him."

"Even if he doesn't exist?"

"Oh, he exists, all right. Somewhere out there"— Emmy gestured dramatically toward the window— "there are two gentlemen just waiting to fall in love with us. And all we need is a little Valentine's magic to get them here."

"A *little* magic? Speak for yourself, Emmy. Personally, I collect it would take more magic than Merlin could come up with to persuade a modern gentleman to fall in love with a penniless female like myself."

"Fustian. It happens all the time."

"When knighthood was in flower perhaps. But in the real world of 1816 it does not work that way.

5

Gentlemen may sigh over and flirt with dowerless young ladies, but when it comes to marriage, they look for a sizable settlement."

"My, you *are* a cynic."

"Not at all. A realist merely. So when I look out that window on St. Valentine's morning it will only be to discover whether or not it's raining. I certainly won't expect Prince Charming on a charger."

"I don't expect him either. For I doubt my odious cousin would know anyone of that nature. But you see, Andrea, I know something that you do not." She paused dramatically. "And what you don't know yet is that it is not only possible, it is most probable that you could see someone from that window who is quite eligible. Now then, Miss Cynic, what have you to say?"

"Merely that, as usual, I have no notion of what you're talking about."

"I know you don't, for I just learned of it this morning. My cousin Blakeney has invited friends from London to hunt here in Berkshire. According to Grandmama, he's taking advantage of his mother's absence to do just as he pleases."

Andrea put down her tambouring to give her friend an incredulous stare. "I'd no idea that your postponed come-out had driven you to desperation, Emmy. You surely don't expect to find the gentleman of your dreams among Lord Blakeney's acquaintances? While I'll admit I have not seen his lordship since we were all children"—indeed, since settling into his lordship's dower house, one of her top priorities had been to avoid any chance encounters with her former tormentor—"you'll not convince me that his character could have done a complete turnabout."

"Oh, lord, no. Blake's as impossible and obnoxious as ever. Why, when I proposed that Grandmama and I should move into the Hall during Lady Blakeney's absence, he wanted to know if I'd been nipping at the port. He said I'd have to be disguised to come up with such a bird-witted notion."

"Well, why did you wish it?" Andrea was genuinely puzzled. "I should think this house much more comfortable than that ancient pile. Why, I remember freezing, not to mention constantly getting lost, when I visited you there in the winter when we were children. I find it much nicer here."

"Nicer? Living in a cramped little box?" Emmy cavalierly dismissed three withdrawing rooms and a library. "And whether or not one freezes is quite beside the point. The fact is, one's consequence is much greater when one is Miss Sedley of Kingswood Hall than merely Miss Sedley of a poky old dower house. And we'd still be living there if Blakeney's overweening, toplofty vixen of a mother had not made it impossible for Grandmama to remain under the same roof with her."

This was an old grievance that Andrea had heard aired often since the two baronesses had ceased speaking to each other several years before. And while her rather hazy memory of the present lord's mother did not contradict Emmy's unflattering description, she still found it difficult to believe that the formidable dowager had not borne her part in any quarrel that had taken place.

"What I've been thinking is," Emmy continued, "that if Blake doesn't choose to have us come and stay, the very least he can do is introduce us to his friends."

"Well, I, for one, desire no such introduction. I

don't wish to cause you distress, dear Emmy, but the very thought of your cousin 'gars me grew,' as my old Scottish nurse would say."

"And what, pray tell, does that mean?"

"Makes me shudder." Andrea demonstrated with a quite realistic fit of the ague. "You surely cannot have forgotten how he used to plague us? Sometimes I felt that even our deep friendship would not survive it."

"Of course I have not forgotten. I'm sure the worst was when he persuaded us to join hands with the parlormaids and take hold of the chain on his electrifying machine without telling us what it was all about. It was horrible, remember?"

"I'm not likely to forget. I was on the end and bore the brunt of the shock."

Emmy giggled suddenly. "And then there was the time when he dropped the frog down the neck of your gown. How old were you then, ten?"

"Thereabouts."

It was a memory that Andrea preferred to keep unresurrected. For worse than the clammy, floppy frog that had sent her shrieking into flight had been the young Lord Blakeney's gallant offer to fish it out and the exploratory time he took in doing so, followed by his crestfallen look of disappointment. Even after so many years, her face flamed at the memory.

"I repeat," she said with renewed firmness, "I have no wish to meet with any of his lordship's friends."

"But that's the amazing thing!" his lordship's cousin exclaimed. "I can't imagine why, but for some reason Blakeney seems to attract gentlemen of the first stare. I can assure you, Andrea, his

8

friends will turn out to be the very pink of the ton. Of course, if he has his way," she said, pouting, "we shall never see them."

But a moment later a smile broke through. "How silly of me. I almost forgot. Blakeney will not be able to prevent us from meeting his London friends."

"Indeed? And whyever not? Do you intend to ask your grandmother to apply pressure on him?"

"Oh, no. That will not be necessary. For once I have put all my Valentine's spells into operation, everything will fall neatly into place. You just wait and see."

Andrea, with great difficulty, suppressed a sigh.

Chapter Two

Yesterday's rain had left the carriage drive muddy and puddle-prone. The young ladies picked their way along it gingerly, their pattens only just elevating their half boots above the muck. "Blake should have this tended to," his lordship's cousin fumed. "And I intend to tell him so."

Then, as if on cue, they heard the pounding of a horse's hooves behind them, galloping furiously as though charging up a hill at Waterloo rather than approaching a tranquil manor house on an overcast winter's morning.

"Oh, no—jump!" Emmy exclaimed. The two young ladies, hitching up their skirts, parted company in the center of the drive to dash to either side.

This maneuver was only partially successful. Whereas they did escape being run down by horse and rider, the gigantic bay hit the deepest puddle at full stride, sending a shower of muddy water arcing out in both directions to descend upon hoods, faces, cloaks, and boots and leaving both ladies speckled and incensed.

"Blake, you ... you ... clodpole!" Emmy screeched at the speeding rider while Andrea fished a handkerchief out of her pocket and began to wipe her face.

The horseman reined in his mount and looked back over his shoulder to study the situation. The smoking bay then wheeled and, at a more sedate pace, approached the fuming ladies.

Andrea watched him warily. At first she thought there was little to be seen of the boy that she had known in the sixth Baron of Kingswood.

Maturity had brought prominent cheekbones into evidence; nor did she recall the slight Wellington arch to his nose. His complexion was weathered to the point that he might have been mistaken for the leader of some Gypsy band instead of the lord of Kingswood Hall. Aiding this impression were the fact that his loose cravat dangled at an open shirt throat and his riding breeches and top boots were even more mud-splattered than her own dark cloak and the fact that he was riding hatless, causing his unkempt dark hair to curl in the dampness at the collar of his riding coat. Andrea could only hope that so great a change in appearance meant a transformation in character as well. But one look into his eyes destroyed that hope. Those eyes were painfully familiar, the same vivid blue she recalled from childhood, sparkling with the same mischievous gleam.

He sat there for several moments, mute and immobile, loftily astride his horse while Emmy sputtered her indignation. Ignoring his fuming cousin completely, his blue eyes, remarkably clear considering his dishabille, looked Andrea up and down. Then, having apparently arrived at some conclusion, his lordship cocked a booted ankle up over the saddle, folded his arms, and relaxed his face into an impish grin. His eyes sparkled with some hidden joke, and Andrea was suddenly ten years old again. To her complete chagrin, she could feel her face turning red.

"Well, well, well. If it ain't the two little furies let loose upon the land again."

"You watch your tongue, Blake. I warn you." His cousin glared up at him. "It's bad enough almost riding us down and splattering us from head to foot—and, by the by, why don't you do something about this drive? It's a disgrace—without reverting to those odious names you used to call us. Harpies. Furies. Hags. How could you?"

"Well, they did seem to fit. Especially furies," he retorted, his grin increasing. "For, as I recall, you were always screeching horrible threats my way and rushing in a pucker here and there. Oh, I say. Did 'gargoyles' get mentioned? Your present expression just happened to bring it to mind, dear Emmy."

Miss Sedley pulled herself up to her inconsiderable height and tried for dignity. "That sort of thing may have done very well for children, Blake. But pray do not start it up again. For though it may have escaped your notice, we've grown up now."

The blue eyes flickered Andrea's way. "I noticed."

"And we're certainly not gargoyles. You might

12

even go so far as to say that we've become diamonds of the first water."

"Hmmm." For a long, uncomfortable moment he studied his cousin and her friend with a connoisseur's eye. "No" was his conclusion. "That's doing it too brown. Though I must admit you two didn't turn out to be the antidotes that I expected." He peered down at his cousin. "Are you still bran-faced, Emmy?"

The very blond Miss Sedley, who was most careful to wear a bonnet in the sun and use liberal amounts of milk of roses and oil of talc, spat back, "I was never bran-faced, and you know it."

"Oh, no? And as for your friend here, let's see now." He leaned over to study Andrea more closely. "The features do well enough. The eyes are quite fine, actually. That is, if you happen to care for large and gray. And the bit of hair sticking out from beneath the hood appears to be the same shiny chestnut that I remember. Yes, she does well enough, actually. Still and all, I'd judge her quite above average but not exceptional enough to be termed a diamond of the first water. "Of course"— the grin widened—"it ain't fair to judge a woman concealed under that tent of a cloak. I could revise my opinion later on."

"It isn't fair for you to judge two *ladies* at all," his cousin retorted. "For it's quite well known that your tastes run to lightskirts."

His eyebrows rose. " 'Ladies' did you say, coz? A true lady turns a blind eye to the . . . er, *diversions*, shall we say . . . of a gentleman. Our mutual grandmother would rap your knuckles for such indelicacy."

"Well, I'm certainly not going to stand on points

13

with you. And I notice you don't deny my accusation. But you are right in one respect. I should not mention your 'diversions,' for I'm not the least bit interested in your whoring."

His lordship recoiled in mock horror, almost unseating himself, and Andrea was moved to whisper "Emmy!" in shocked protest.

"Well, I'm not. Interested, that is. And I'm certainly not going to waste my time preaching propriety to you."

"I can't begin to tell you how that relieves me," his lordship informed the threatening sky.

"For the fact is, I have matters of far greater importance to discuss with you. We were on our way to the Hall to do so."

"We were?" Andrea blurted out indignantly. "But you told me that . . ." She stopped herself in midsentence.

"Do I sense some reluctance on your part to pay me a morning call, Miss Prior? I'm wounded. For I remember *you* most fondly."

"You do nothing of the sort," Andrea retorted. "And as for any reluctance on my part, I was merely going to point out that I'd no idea that Emeline wished to discuss some matter with you. I would not dream of intruding in family affairs."

"Well, you can shelve your sensibilities. Emmy and I don't *discuss*. She demands and I say no. End of exchange." His bay began to move restlessly, impatiently sniffing the stables. "So shall we consider it done, little cousin? I'll not keep Horatio standing."

"Go on then and see to your horse by all means. Though it does seem a shame that you can't show the same consideration for your family that you do your cattle."

"But it's nothing to wonder at, is it? For my cattle don't go on and on at a fellow. And they're never into my purse the way that you are, Emmy."

"Well, if you weren't so clutch-fisted, I wouldn't need to—"

"Clutch-fisted?" he interrupted. "Most would say I've been more than generous." The blue eyes were beginning to look rather flinty.

"Well, if anyone thinks that, it only goes to show they haven't the slightest notion of the real needs of a young lady ready to take her place in society. I need more than money from you, Blake."

"Oh, God."

"No need to take that tone. My requests are not likely to cause you inconvenience."

"You can be deuced sure of that."

"There you go again." Emmy's voice broke and her eyes grew moist with the threat of tears. "Prejudging before you even hear what I have to say. Oh, why, oh, why do I have to be dependent upon you for every breath I take? It simply is not fair."

"Fair? What's fair got to say to anything? And if you're planning to turn on the fountains, coz, I'll advise you not to. Your tears won't move me. For if there's one thing I despise, it's a weepy female. What's more, they're likely to freeze out here."

"You really are a heartless knave, Blake. Go on. Stable your precious horse. Andrea and I will meet you in your library. I am resolved that for once we shall have a sensible talk. What's more, I shall not allow you to get me up in arms. For I am quite determined to force you to see reason."

"The day that I give in to your notion of reason,

Emmy m'dear, is the day they straitjacket me. But if we must have our little scene, so be it. Only we'll have it in the breakfast room. Tell Higgens I'm famished."

He wheeled his horse abruptly. It could have been merely by accident that the huge bay reared, then brought his hooves crashing down in the selfsame mud puddle that had showered them before. While his cousin screeched invective at his rapidly retreating back, Lord Blakeney waved mockingly to them over his shoulder.

The young ladies trudged toward Kingswood Hall in uncharacteristic silence. The bare oaks that overlapped the drive with dank, dark limbs against a matching sky did nothing to elevate their spirits. Emmy seemed intent on banking her fury, a piece of self-restraint that Andrea found amazing and secretly applauded. She herself was rather out of countenance with her friend for duping her into a visit with his loathsome lordship. It did not help her state of mind when they rounded a bend in the driveway and she caught her first glimpse in years of his stately residence.

Andrea had hoped that time and maturity would have erased the awe that edifice had formerly evoked in her. They had not. She might have been a child again, so intimidating did she find the ancient pile.

But she was not a child, she reminded herself as they made their way up the circular drive, and she tried to analyze just why this particular house affected her in this way. Certainly she had visited far grander. Nor was Kingswood Hall a thing of beauty. It was constructed as a single, enormous block of a once light-colored stone that had since become time-darkened. There was no break in its facade, no extended wings to lend it distinction. A small flight of stone steps, flanked by an undistinguished balustrade, led upward to a heavy oaken door, which was devoid of any pediment. The basically unimaginative architecture was partially rescued, however, by a noble roof, which was hipped and lit with dormer windows, punctuated by massive chimney stacks, and surmounted by a handsome cupola.

It was the very solidity of Kingswood Hall, its sense of permanence, that she found so overweening, Andrea concluded. It seemed to mock her own fly-by-night existence and throw her rootless status in her face.

My lineage is the equal of the Blakeneys', if not better, she reminded herself firmly. It did not help. Being the daughter of the black sheep of a noble line played havoc with one's sense of consequence.

Emmy sniffed and stared around her as they were ushered into the great hall by the ancient butler, who had taken his time about answering their summons. Judging from a telltale egg stain at the corner of his disapproving mouth, he had been interrupted at a late breakfast.

"Well, it's quite plain that Blake is allowing this place to go to rack and ruin." Emmy's words were directed to Andrea, but the butler was obviously the intended target. "I vow those marbles have not seen a feather duster since my aunt left for London." She gestured at the classical statuary set within decorative niches that marched around the walls. "And as for this floor . . ." Words failed her, but the muddy boot marks on the black-and-white-checkered marble spoke for themselves. "Just wait till I tell Grandmama of the state things are in here."

Andrea did not think it her imagination that the butler paled a bit beneath the salt-and-pepper stubble on his unshaven face. And in his eagerness to comply with Miss Sedley's order that Lord Blakeney's breakfast be prepared immediately, he came close to fawning.

The ladies had barely seated themselves in the breakfast parlor when they heard his lordship's footsteps. And it became immediately obvious that he'd made no modifications in his toilet. The odor of the stables preceded him.

"Well, if it isn't 'Beau' Blakeney himself." Emmy's voice was heavily sarcastic.

"That's the thanks I get for not making you cool your heels while I changed? There are enough fops in this world without me swelling their numbers." He took his place at the head of the breakfast table, whereupon one footman filled his cup with the tea from a steaming silver pot and another placed a heaping plateful of food before him.

"Small chance of anyone accusing you of foppishness, dear cousin." Emmy took a place at the table, uninvited, and motioned Andrea to join her while she poured out from his lordship's teapot for both of them. "But is it too much to expect you to dress like a gentleman?"

"Did you trudge all this way simply to ring a peal over me, Emmy?" his lordship inquired through a mouthful of cold mutton. "If so, it was a wasted trip.

"By the by, Miss Prior, to what do we owe the honor of your visit? As I recall, you were mostly used to coming with the robins and the apple blossoms and all those other harbingers of spring. Oh, the devil!" For a moment he actually looked disconcerted. "I forgot. Your father's hared off to the Continent to escape the hounds, hasn't he? You *had* to come here."

"Blakeney!" His cousin was glaring at him furiously. "You are the most complete, insensitive clodpole!"

"Never mind, Emmy." Andrea's color had heightened a bit, but her voice was well under control and icily haughty. "One neither expects nor desires an excess of tact from Lord Blakeney. But since your lordship has brought up the subject, it is true that my father left England—suddenly—and put me temporarily in the care of your grandmother. I shall be joining him in France as soon as he's settled."

"I see."

Blakeney's voice was noncommittal, but Andrea had no doubt that he had drawn his own conclusions.

Emmy, possibly recalling some past bit of sage advice concerning flies, honey, and vinegar, gave her cousin an artificial smile. "At least it was good of you to take note of the fact that this is a dreadful place to visit in the wintertime."

"Is that what I said?" Blakeney reached for a light wig and buttered it liberally.

"It's what you implied when you mentioned how surprising it is that Andrea did not time her visit with the apple blossoms. It's obvious that you were thinking of how dull things must be here for her. Which is most considerate of you, Blake."

"Get to the point, Emmy, and let me do the buttering." He popped a generous portion of the roll into his mouth.

"Very well. The *point*, cousin, is that we are both perishing from boredom."

Andrea opened her mouth to object to such an inclusion but quickly closed it again at her friend's warning look.

"That shows a rather pathetic want of resourcefulness, cousin. Have you tried all of those things females are always doing? Nightmares in watercolors. Netted purses that could be used as feed bags. Vocal exercises that set the dogs ahowl. The usual female accomplishments."

"I'm not speaking of that kind of thing. We stand in need of society."

"Then ask the vicar's wife to tea. I hear she's the biggest gossipmonger in the county. You should get enough scandal from her to chew on for a fortnight."

"That's not the kind of society I'm referring to and you perfectly well know it. And you have no right to try to make light of the fact that I am simply wasting away here when I should be making my bow in London."

"Oh, God." His lordship groaned and pushed back his emptied plate, which the hovering footman deftly removed. "Spare me your come-out again, Emmy. All that's been settled. You'll go next year. Lord knows I wanted you to go this Season. Nobody is more eager than I to have you hook some poor, unsuspecting sapskull and be off my hands."

"If that's so, why didn't you make the town house available?"

"As far as I'm concerned, the town house is and always has been available."

"It is not. Your mother is ensconced there."

"It's a big house." His lordship's voice was wearied with the well-worn argument. "There is plenty of room for all. And for all the balls and assemblies—whatever—that you'd care to give."

"No house is big enough for both Grandmama and your mother."

"True. But I'm hardly to blame for that. Nor am I at fault because Grandmama wouldn't allow my mother to bring you out."

"You know perfectly well that Grandmama is determined to sponsor my come-out."

"I know it now." He sighed. "But for God's sake, Emmy, show a little patience. I've made it clear to Mama that you're to have full run of the place next Season. If necessary, I'll send her packing to the Continent. Though why I have to resort to such extreme measures I'll never understand. Females!" Blakeney reached for the port decanter in disgust. "Anyhow," he continued after a gulp that drained half the glass, "you will make your come-out, Emmy. And since you're barely out of leading strings, I see no need for you to make such a Cheltenham tragedy over a year's delay."

"Because there is absolutely nothing to do here, that's why," his cousin wailed. "And since it's your fault that I'm wasting away here— Yes, it is." She cut off his protest before he could utter it. "For you should have known that Grandmama and my aunt are at daggers drawn and are both too stubborn to compromise on my account. So it's up to you to do something to make my life less miserable here and now."

"Aren't you being rather insulting to Miss Prior here? It's hard to imagine being miserable in such company. By the by, the cloak did conceal a lot. I may be forced to reevaluate the rating I gave you earlier." The smile he gave Andrea was not far removed from a leer. At least it was close enough to cause her to bristle. His lordship chuckled softly at her reaction.

"Though she is far too well bred to admit it," Emmy plowed on, oblivious to the exchange, "I am sure that Andrea is bored to distraction as well. That is why you must give a hunt ball, Blake."

His lordship strangled on his second, more modest mouthful of port. "Give a *what*?" he exclaimed when he'd recovered.

"You heard me perfectly."

"I can't possibly have done so, for I could swear you mentioned a *hunt* ball, which customarily follows a *hunt*, in case you haven't heard, my sap-skulled cousin."

"What I've heard—what I *know*—is that you've invited some friends down here for a hunt."

"Actually, they invited themselves. But that's neither here nor there. Four coves coursing after rabbits does not constitute a hunt. But that's neither here nor there either. For even if it were the Quorn itself, I would not give a ball for your amusement, little cousin, so get that particular maggot out of your brain."

"That's mean-spirited, Blakeney!"

"So be it."

"It's not as if you'd be in the least discommoded. Grandmama and Andrea and I would see to everything. Why, we could move up here beforehand to make it easier and—"

"No!"

Blakeney slapped his hand down on the table,

setting his cup and saucer adance. "Stop it right now, Emeline. Three friends of mine are coming here for a few days of peaceful shooting. And they are coming here precisely because this is a bachelor establishment, with no hectoring females to spoil the fun. There will be no balls at Kingswood. Get that into your head. Nor are my friends to be considered as prime catches, is that clear? Keep your distance, Emmy. If you want a party, give one. But at the dower house. And don't bother to direct any cards this way."

"You selfish beast!" Emmy pushed back her chair angrily. "Why I have to be saddled with such a heartless, slovenly lecher of a guardian, I'll never know."

"Nor why I have to have such a sweet, biddable ward. But it's an unjust world, dear cousin."

"Come, Andrea. I'm sorry I had to subject you to such a scene. The truth is, you see, that I constantly keep hoping that my cousin's meanness might improve. But as you can see, he is still essentially the same odious brat who dropped the frog inside your gown."

"Did I actually do that?" His lordship grinned broadly as Andrea rose. "Ah, yes. Now I do recall. But come to think on it, I wasn't a total villain, now, was I? For I distinctly remember that I also fished it out."

His grin widened as Andrea felt her face grow hot.

Chapter
Three

Even after the friends had reached the dower house, Emmy refused to simmer down. She paced about their bedchamber angrily, calling her cousin every unflattering name allowed on a lady's tongue and a few more that were of questionable propriety.

"Perhaps it's just as well he takes that attitude," Andrea said placatingly. "I, for one, am as happy to avoid him as he is us. He really doesn't care much for females, does he?"

"Humph!" Lord Blakeney's cousin snorted. "He cares for females of a certain stamp right enough. Wasn't it obvious when we met that he'd just come from whoring?"

"Emmy! You must stop using that particular term."

"Why wrap the matter up in clean linen? He'd

spent the night with some barmaid or tinker's daughter—who knows what sort of low creature. Oh, my cousin is quite fond of *females*. It's just *ladies* he avoids like the plague.

"Of course"—she had stopped her pacing to occupy the window seat and was beginning to calm down a bit—"I hold my grandmother and my aunt partially to blame for his attitude."

"Well, yes," Andrea said, resuming her needlework, "I can see that their feuding might give him a certain distaste for our gender."

"That, too. But I was referring to the fact that they are both quite determined to find him a wife. They're rivals in that as in all else. Each wants a daughter completely under her thumb, don't you see."

Andrea did see. And for the first time in her life, perhaps, she felt a stir of sympathy for Lord Blakeney. It quickly passed.

"Which is all the more reason"—Emmy refused to be long diverted from her grievance—"that he should have consented to give a ball. He would have a chance to be with suitable young ladies without his mother's interference."

"There's still your grandmother, however," Andrea reminded her.

"True. But he can get around her easily enough. Of course, to be perfectly honest, he doesn't pay the slightest attention to his mother's scheming either." Emmy was rapidly rekindling. "No, Blakeney is entirely selfish and refuses to bother himself for anyone. Oh, I quite long to give him a severe setdown. I should love to puncture that conceit. I would like to make him realize just how odious . . ."

She paused suddenly in her diatribe. A wicked

smile lit up her face and she clapped her hands in delight. "I know what to do, Andrea. It's the very thing. We'll make him a valentine."

"Send Blakeney a valentine? Isn't that the very opposite of the sentiments you've been expressing?"

"Oh, not a valentine's valentine. A nasty one. Nasty-comic, that is. Something to burst the bubble of his conceit. People send that sort of thing all the time. There are actually books of comic verses you can buy. The Cruikshanks who do those wicked political drawings also go in for insulting valentines. But, more's the pity, we haven't time to send away for anything. We shall have to do our own. You're good at rhyming, Andrea. So you be thinking while I collect the materials we'll need to make the card."

Andrea wasn't sure she wanted to be a party to such a scheme, but when Emmy returned, armed with paper, scissors, paints, paste, and bits of lace and ribbon, her sense of mischief had gotten the better of her and she was seated at the writing table deep in thought while she tickled her nose with the quill's feather.

Emmy went down on her knees before the fireplace and spread her materials around. "I'll decorate the front of the folder first, something quite sentimental so he'll think he's getting a real billet-doux. I wonder if I can draw a cupid."

There was a period of silence broken only by the scratching of the quill and the occasional clinking of a watercolor brush upon a glass's rim. "Oh, bother!" Emmy picked up the folder and frowned at it critically. "My cupids look like flying pigs armed with bows and arrows."

"Well, it's supposed to be a comic valentine, is it not?" Andrea asked.

"But he's not to discover that until he reads the verse. Oh, well." She sighed. "Perhaps I'd best confine myself to red hearts and blue forget-me-nots."

Silence reigned once more. Then: "Oh, I say! This is beginning to look quite pretty. Pity to waste it, actually. How are you coming?"

"I'm not sure. What do you think?" Andrea picked up her paper, held it dramatically at arm's length, and declaimed:

> "My dear Lord Blakeney—
>
> Cock of the Walk, you rule the roost
> As though you were divine.
> But despite both rank and fortune
> You are no one's Valentine."

"Well, it could be nastier" was Emmy's judgment. "But, still, it should put the conceited jackanapes in his proper place."

"Of course, there is one problem."

"And what is that?"

"He is certain to know we sent it."

"Oh, no, he won't." Emmy chuckled evilly. "Oh, he'll suspect us, of course. But the thing is, you see, we will be only two of dozens of suspects. For you would be amazed at the number of well-bred females my cousin has given reason to echo our sentiments. Oh, this will drive him wild. I've not the slightest doubt of it. I cannot believe what a famous idea I have come up with!"

But, later on, Andrea began to have second thoughts concerning their creative efforts. Indeed, the whole thing now struck her as childish in the extreme. It vexed her to think that a single encounter with the grown-up Lord Blakeney could thrust her back into a ten-year-old's mentality. She strove to regain some sense of maturity and dignity, for she had just been informed by her ladyship's maid that her mistress wished to speak to her.

She was ushered into the dowager baroness's bedchamber and seated in a carved gilt armchair near the august presence. Lady Blakeney was busy at her secretary and did not bother to glance up as she spoke. "I shall only be a moment." She dipped her quill into the inkpot and added a flourishing signature to the letter she'd been writing. While her ladyship was carefully sprinkling sand to dry the ink, Andrea studied her covertly.

Perhaps it was the close-fitting white cap with its broad bands hugging the cheeks and supporting the sagging chin that made Andrea think of coifs. The severe black gown her ladyship wore also added to the nunlike effect. It occurred to her that Lady Blakeney would have made an excellent Mother Superior. Not that Andrea had any clear notion of the qualities necessary for such a lofty position. But she did know quite well that Lady Blakeney should be in charge of something.

Despite her small stature, which one quickly forgot since her ladyship refused to yield even a fraction of an inch to age by stooping, she had a commanding presence. An autocratic presence, actually, which was intensified by an aquiline nose and piercing black eyes. Yes, clearly she was born to rule. A pity she could not usurp the inept regent. Certainly the dower house did not allow her sufficient scope. No wonder she had parted from the Hall with such a lack of grace.

The letter disposed of, the gimlet eyes fastened speculatively upon Andrea. That young lady managed, barely, not to quail. "Meg said you wished to see me, Lady Blakeney," she remarked unnecessarily.

"Yes. I think it time we considered your future, Andrea."

Andrea felt her hackles begin to rise. "It's most kind of your ladyship to feel concerned. But you need not trouble yourself on my account. My father will be sending for me shortly. And then I shall keep house in France for him. I do hope I have not outstayed my welcome here."

"Humph!" The dowager's frown was imperious. "No need to adopt that hoity-toity tone, miss. And of course you have not outstayed your welcome. But the fact of the matter is that while you are under my roof I feel a responsibility for you. And I do not intend to mince my words. Plain speaking is always the best course, as I long ago discovered. So I hope you will take what I am going to say in the proper spirit. This is for your own good." Her ladyship paused. Since she clearly expected some utterance, Andrea managed a feeble "Yes, ma'am."

"Well, then, that is settled. What I think you must do, Andrea, is to face up to a few home truths. The first of which is that your father, while a handsome, well-born charmer, possesses a fatal flaw. He is an addicted gambler."

"Now, really, Lady Blakeney." Andrea, her face aflame, started to rise. Lady Blakeney reached for the ebony and silver walking stick she always carried, more as a badge of authority than for support, and gently pushed her back down into her chair with it. "I warned you not to allow yourself to get into a taking, child. Now hear me out.

"Your charming father, whom you doubtlessly and rightly adore, is a gambler. He has squandered his fortune in the gaming halls of London and has been forced to take up residence on the Continent to escape his creditors. Now he himself, like all gamblers, is convinced that his reverses are only temporary. My fear is that he has also convinced you of this." She paused again.

Andrea held her head high. "Papa has been under the hatches before and has always come about."

"And may do so again," her ladyship conceded. "And if so, what will happen?"

"He plans to buy a house just outside of Paris where we can live more economically. And, as I said, he will then send for me."

"And never approach a gaming table again?" the dowager asked dryly.

"Well, as for that, I couldn't say."

"Oh, can you not, Andrea? I have known you all your life and never thought you lacked for sense. I collect that, even though you may not have acknowledged the fact, deep down you yourself must realize that your father is addicted to gaming in the same way that some men—and women, for that matter—take to spirits. And the leopard does not change its spots or the gambler his habits.

"Now I realize that you think me a cruel monster for speaking thus and forcing you to face facts that can only cause you pain. But the sooner you come to realize, m'dear, that you must rely upon yourself and leave your father to go to perdition in his own fashion, the better off you will be. Have you thought about your future, Andrea? I mean beyond your papa's pipe dreams."

"Well, yes, I have." Andrea met the dowager's questioning gaze squarely. "I plan to give English lessons. When Papa gets our house."

"I see." Her ladyship's voice was expressionless, but a wry smile acknowledged the hit. "Tell me. Have you ever considered teaching French to the English instead?"

"Yes, I have, actually. And if Papa doesn't send for me in a few weeks' time, I shall apply for a position as a governess."

"No!"

If she had hoped to impress Lady Blakeney with such forethought, she was disappointed. Her ladyship disposed of "governess" with a thump of her stick. "That will not do. A girl with your background and temperament would loathe being confined to one household, treated little better than an upper servant, and most likely saddled with unspeakable brats who have little aptitude or desire to learn. And, given your good looks, you are bound to fall prey to attempts at seduction by the master of the house or by any sons who are old enough to try to get underneath your skirts."

"Really, Lady Blakeney."

"No need to turn missish. Plain speaking, remember? Unwelcome advances of a sexual nature are apt to be the lot of any young governess who is not as plain as a pikestaff.

"No, a governess's position will not do. Nor will my original idea, which was to employ you as my companion. It seemed sensible at first. Emeline will soon be leaving. But there is no need to look aghast, m'dear. I dismissed that idea myself. For I knew

31

you would hate it above all things. It was then that I came up with the perfect solution. You must open your own school."

There was a lengthy pause. Then she asked, "Well, Andrea, what do you have to say for yourself?"

"Merely that such a course of action is outside of my capabilities, ma'am."

"Nonsense. You must not underrate yourself. You are certainly as good a scholar as that academic charlatan Miss Wadsworth, whose overpriced academy you and Emeline attended."

"You misunderstand me, Lady Blakeney. It's not my scholastic ability I refer to. While I'll admit that the notion of establishing my own school has occurred to me and is appealing, it would require a great deal of capital. And, as you've just observed, money is a problem with my father at the moment. But when he gets his affairs in order again, I shall certainly consider—"

The dowager interrupted with a jarring thump of her stick. "Your father has nothing to say in this matter. That is what I have been trying to drive into your head, child. I have given your situation a great deal of thought and I see no reason why you should not open a school right here. There are enough prosperous farmers around here whose wives have aspirations above their stations to furnish you with sufficient pupils to begin with. I thought you should start in a small way. With day pupils. Then, if things go well, as I am convinced they will, you can gradually take on boarding students."

"But I don't see—"

"Of course you do not," her ladyship barked.

"Pray allow me to finish. Blakeney has an empty cottage now, since one of our pensioners has recently died. The place would be quite suitable for a beginning school and there is no reason you should not use it."

"You have discussed the matter with Lord Blakeney then?"

"I have not yet informed him of my plan. But I can assure you that my grandson has every reason to want to comply with my wishes. He owes me that much consideration for allowing That Woman to have her complete way in other matters. No, Blakeney will not object."

"What is it that Blake will not object to?"

Miss Emeline Sedley, wearing a heavy cloak and pattens, entered the room. "I can't imagine what you are discussing so seriously, but I'll bet a monkey that my odious cousin will object to anything that anyone else wishes."

"Not to this. We were discussing Andrea's future. And do refrain from using cant phrases, Emeline. And do not call your cousin odious."

Emmy ignored the rebuke and went straight to the heart of the matter. "What about Andrea's future, Grandmama?"

She listened impatiently while her grandmother once again outlined her plan. "You should go look at the cottage right away, Andrea," the dowager concluded. "I think you will agree that it is most suitable."

"Well, no harm in looking, I suppose." Emmy displayed a notable lack of enthusiasm. "In fact, if there's time, we can go today. I was coming to see if you'd like to walk with me, Andrea. That is, if you and Grandmama are quite finished. But I can tell you now, seeing the cottage will be a complete waste of your time."

"Indeed?" Her ladyship's eyebrows rose alarmingly. But the look she bent upon her granddaughter failed to intimidate that irrepressible young lady.

"Oh, yes, indeed. For oddly enough Andrea and I also have been discussing our futures. And while opening a school might do very well for some platter-faced bluestocking, it will not do for Andrea. No, she must find a husband. A husband is the only solution to both of our difficulties."

"Indeed?" The dowager's tone increased in frigidity. "While I realize that that is the popular notion for an eighteen-year-old flibbertigibbet to hold, I must tell you that a husband, seen from a seventy-year-old's perspective, is quite unlikely to be the solution to any difficulty. A husband, in my experience, is far more likely to become the problem."

Chapter
Four

As they set out on their walk, Andrea had to admit that valentine creation had had a cathartic effect upon Emmy. They were carrying baskets of delicacies to an elderly servant who had been pensioned off to one of the estate cottages. As they trudged along in the cold, Emmy was swinging her basket back and forth to the peril of its contents and humming a lively tune to herself. Her mood change seemed quite in keeping with the heavens, which had decided to burst forth into sunshine at almost the last possible moment after having glowered all through the day. Andrea decided to keep her own second thoughts to herself and not destroy Emmy's cheerfulness. She could always persuade her friend not to post the hateful valentine to her cousin when the time for such a final action came.

Her thoughts were interrupted by the sound of

carriage wheels. The girls abandoned the driveway for the verge and stared with frank curiosity as a crested traveling coach drew abreast. In response to a shout from the interior of the carriage the coachman reined in his pair, and the head and shoulders of a modern-day Adonis leaned out the window.

He doffed his curly-brimmed beaver to reveal fair hair attractively arranged in a Titus crop. His sky blue eyes lit up in appreciation as he gazed at the young ladies, and his smile, revealing white, even teeth, was most disarming. "I do beg your pardon, but could you tell me if we are on the right road to Kingswood Hall?"

"Well, no, not quite." Emmy dimpled back at the contagious smile. "When the road forked a half-mile back, you should have taken the left branch, not the right."

"Did I not tell you so?" The Adonis turned back into the coach's interior. "You and your curst coin toss, Gresham. Still"—he redirected his gaze and charm out the window once again—"I cannot regret the error. It's worth prolonging our tedious journey for the sight of two such visions wandering the countryside. Tell me, is this what we can expect of Berkshire? Will all the young ladies we meet here be goddesses?"

Andrea was beginning to find the attractive young man too fulsome by half and nudged Emmy, indicating they should walk on.

Her friend ignored the hint. "Your question is academic, sir," she replied quite seriously. "For if my cousin has his way, you'll have no basis for comparison."

"Your cousin!" the young man exclaimed. He was

36

opening the coach door and climbing out. "Don't tell me that you are Blake's cousin. Why, that sly old dog! He never mentioned that he had a cousin who was a diamond of the first water."

Emmy shot Andrea a look of triumph at the term.

"Oh, I say, we are well met. Let me introduce myself—and my friends as well, it seems," he added as his two companions also left the coach to join the party at the roadside. He gestured toward the gentleman who had emerged first. "This, er, portly, distinguished-looking fellow is Lord Gresham."

"Portly" was a charitable description, Andrea thought. "Fat" would have put it in a nutshell. It was not this attribute that she found unattractive, though. It was the small, piglike eyes and the peevish expression that repelled her. His lordship nodded perfunctorily at the introduction. He was obviously impatient to finish his journey.

"And this shy young fellow," the spokesman continued in a teasing tone, "is Sir Nigel Lyncomb."

A young man of medium build, brown hair and eyes, and a pleasant face peered around Lord Gresham's bulk, lifted his hat, and bowed their way. "H-how do you do?" he stammered.

"And I, fair cousin of Lord Blakeney, am Mr. Beau Austen, at your service. And"—he focused the dazzling smile upon Andrea—"are you another cousin that our dog-in-the-manger host has kept a secret?"

Andrea, though not nearly as impervious to the young man's charm as she might have wished, still managed to reply with sufficient reserve that she hoped would balance Emmy's forwardness. "No, I am not."

"Oh, this is my dear friend, Miss Prior." Emmy

might have been a hostess in a drawing room. "And I am Miss Sedley."

The three gentlemen acknowledged the introductions. Gresham was perfunctory, Sir Nigel bashful, and Mr. Austen extravagant. "Since we're already on the wrong road entirely, may we convey you ladies to wherever you're going with those heavy baskets?" Mr. Austen concluded.

"Oh, I say!" Gresham muttered under his breath.

Andrea spoke quickly before Emmy could accept. "Thank you very much, sir, but we are bent on exercise. Besides," she added to soften the effect of her repressive tone, "I'm sure Lord Blakeney is most eager for your arrival."

"Oh, well." Mr. Austen sighed, then quickly brightened. "At least we're certain to meet again. Only whatever did you mean," he asked Emmy, "that we'd have no basis for comparison among you and the other young women hereabouts?"

"Merely that my selfish cousin means to keep you entirely to himself."

"Why, the scoundrel. But he'll find that an impossible task with two such lovely ladies living at the manor house. And as for meeting other young ladies in the neighborhood, we will have no desire to make comparisons."

"Oh, but we do not live at the manor house."

Mr. Austen's expression changed to one of appropriate dismay. "You don't? How dreadful."

"No, we're stuck in the fusty old dower house. You would have passed it about a half-mile beyond the gate."

"Why, yes, come to think on it, I did notice chimney stacks amongst the trees. Well, at least we shall be neighbors. We'll arrange for dear old Blake to introduce us properly."

"I can assure you he will not," Miss Sedley replied bluntly.

"Emmy, really!" Andrea protested between her teeth.

"My cousin is quite determined to do nothing but slaughter poor innocent rabbits while you are here. I tried to persuade him to give a ball for your entertainment, but he wouldn't hear of it."

"What a curmudgeon! Why, a ball would be the very thing."

"Mustn't keep the horses standing, Beau," Lord Gresham remarked pointedly. And with a token tip of his hat he climbed back into the carriage.

Mr. Austen's rueful smile was intended to cover his friend's rudeness. "He's right, of course. We shouldn't keep the horses standing in this cold. But our meeting has been most fortuitous, ladies. For I'm beginning to suspect that Blake intended to keep your very existence a secret. But the cat's out of the bag now. And you may be assured we'll meet again. Ladies." He bowed elegantly, Sir Nigel shyly, and then both joined their companion in the coach. Then, as the coachman cracked his whip, Mr. Austen flashed his gleaming smile out of the window once again. "And be assured, Miss Sedley, we shall have that ball. I give you my solemn word on it."

As they left the park and entered the farmland lying fallow in the February cold, Emmy seemed to walk on air. Her eyes shone. She chattered incessantly. Every feature and word of Mr. Austen were recalled and analyzed. He was then pronounced to be the very epitome of the ideal gentleman. "Did I not say that Blake's friends would prove to be exceptional?" she crowed.

Andrea conceded that Mr. Austen certainly was capable of making a favorable first impression, though whether he would wear well was another matter, she qualified to her friend's disgust. But, in point of fact, she had found Lord Gresham anything but exceptional. "Churlish" would be a more fitting description. "As for Sir—Nigel, was it?—I was entirely unable to form an opinion of that young man. He appeared quite as retiring as your Mr. Austen was forward."

"He wasn't *my* Mr. Austen," Emmy protested unconvincingly. "He looked at you at least as much as he looked at me. And he called us both diamonds."

"No, Emmy, you were the only diamond. I merely obtained 'lovely.' Do you suppose he terms all females whom he happens to meet on wealthy country estates nonpareils?"

"Don't be absurd. He couldn't, could he? In most cases it simply would not fit."

Andrea smothered a smile at her friend's conceit while Emmy went on to plan enthusiastically for a ball at Kingswood. When to hold it. Whom to invite. What to wear.

"Aren't you being premature? I doubt that Mr. Austen can change your cousin's mind."

"Of course he can. Didn't Blake refuse me because he thought his guests would not like it? Once Mr. Austen assures him that he mistakes the matter, why, he's bound to come around."

Andrea doubted that very much. She was convinced that Lord Blakeney arranged his life entirely for his own convenience. But she kept this opinion to herself. It was good to have Emmy in high spirits once again. If the bubble had to be burst, let his lordship be the one to do it.

They turned off the wagon road onto a lane that led to a tiny cottage half hidden behind an enormous lime. As they approached, the door opened and a young man strode rapidly out and down the path.

He was rudely dressed in a short jacket, knee breeches, and leggings. But there was nothing subservient in his mien or in the hard look he gave the two approaching ladies.

There was something familiar about him, Andrea thought as they drew nearer. He was of average height and medium frame with classical facial features. Not a person easily forgotten, she concluded. Nor will he forget us soon, she added to herself with some annoyance as the gray eyes took their measure.

He reached the gate first and opened it. The civil thing would have been to step aside and allow the young ladies to enter. Instead he shut the gate behind him with a firm click and passed them on the path without so much as a nod in their direction.

I'll wager he's never pulled a forelock in his life, Andrea thought, more annoyed than she would have admitted. "Who was that?" she whispered to Emmy as they opened the gate for themselves.

"Him?" Emmy was obviously still preoccupied with the London visitors. She glanced back over her shoulder at the rapidly retreating form. "Oh, that must be Molly's grandson. He grew up here, but I thought he'd gone away for good."

The subject held no interest for her, and Andrea, too, soon dismissed the churlish young man from her mind. They delivered their baskets, drank the obligatory cups of tea, and listened to the neighborhood gossip, which did not include any reference to a visiting grandson and was passed on with relish by the dowager's former cook. Molly Cannon was a wizened elderly woman, who, though a victim of rheumatism, the crippling effects of which made her movements painful even to watch, seemed to have retained a remarkable zest for life. She enjoyed their visit prodigiously and successfully blocked several attempts on their part to bring it to a close.

The two young ladies were forced to walk rapidly back home to escape the dark. As it was, their dinner awaited them.

While they ate, Emmy eagerly told her grandmother every minute detail of their encounter with the London visitors. The dowager listened intently but did not offer any comment, not even when Emmy related Mr. Austen's promise of a ball.

Miss Sedley needed no encouragement, however. She wore the subject threadbare throughout the evening while Andrea tried to read and Lady Blakeney was engaged in needlework. It lasted through tea without any noticeable flagging of interest on Emmy's part. It was only as she and Andrea prepared for bed that the spate was temporarily diverted. She paused in the act of pulling on her nightcap. "Oh, my heavens! I forgot the eggs!"

Andrea thought her friend daft and said so. "What do you want with eggs after all we've eaten? You can't possibly be hungry."

"I'm *not* hungry. The eggs aren't for eating. Well, they are, of course, but that's not the point. Don't go to bed yet. I'll be right back. I asked Cook to boil two eggs for us."

Andrea was slowly rotating in front of the fire trying to heat her nightdress before crawling into the chilly bed, which was as far removed from the fireplace as the bedchamber allowed, when Emmy hurried back into the room. In her hands were two boiled eggs and a bunch of dried bay leaves. "Here, eat this." She thrust an egg toward Andrea.

"But I told you, I'm stuffed," the other protested.

"And I told you that hunger or the lack of it has nothing to say in the matter. It's a Valentine's custom that Grandmama told me about. If we eat a hard-boiled egg just before bedtime and pin five bay leaves to our pillows, we'll dream of the men we shall marry.

"Well, actually, we are supposed to do it on Valentine's eve, but I don't see why, as long as we do it in the proper spirit, it should not work now just as well."

"Oh, I'm certain it will. Every bit as well," Andrea said dryly.

"For I expect that the egg and the bay leaves have more to do with it than the actual date, don't you?" Emmy stooped to crack her egg upon the hearth.

"Undoubtedly." Andrea followed suit, peeling her egg and tossing the shells into the flames. "Indigestion should guarantee the dreams."

Much later that night she was running down a long, winding driveway in pursuit of a speeding carriage, screaming, "Papa! Papa! Please don't go. Don't leave me, Papa!" and she was not in the least surprised to discover that she was a child once more. Tears were streaming down her cheeks as the traveling coach left her farther and farther behind. Then, miracle of miracles, the carriage began to slow down and down. It then stopped altogether.

"Papa!" Andrea increased her speed. "Papa, you waited after all!" She raced up to the carriage where a window light was lowered and a tall man in a curly beaver stretched his arms out toward her.

She was just about to allow herself to be pulled upward through the window when she suddenly froze in horror. "But you aren't Papa!" The mocking face, laughing down at her, was Lord Blakeney's.

Andrea rolled over, pricked her cheek on a pinned bay leaf, and sat bolt upright.

"You're freezing me, Andrea. What is the matter?" Emmy's muffled voice complained.

"Nothing." Andrea lay back down and rearranged the covers to keep the drafts off. "I have just had a nightmare, that's all."

Chapter
Five

*T*he *next morning the postman brought a letter*
from Andrea's father. She excused herself and
left the breakfast table. In the privacy of her bedchamber she broke the seal and read the single page
once, twice, and a third time for good measure,
fighting all the while to hold back the tears.

Her father wrote that he had had some recent
financial reverses and, as a result, would not be
able to send for her as soon as he had hoped. In the
meantime he was comforted to know that she was
in the company of her dearest friend and therefore
would not feel the separation too keenly. He could
assure her that it would not be long before they
were reunited. He had several schemes in mind
that were certain to bring a turnabout in his fortunes. In the meantime he remained "her most
affectionate father."

She sat motionless on the window seat for several minutes gazing out into space. Try as she might to hold them at bay, Lady Blakeney's words, "addicted gambler," came back to mock her. She hadn't the slightest doubt as to what the dowager would make of her father's "financial reverses." The only question would be, Was it cards or the faro table?

A wave of bitterness swept through her. She struggled to overcome it. Nor would she indulge in a bout of self-pity. She squared her shoulders. She simply had to shake off the last of her childish dependency and learn to rely upon herself.

And Lady Blakeney had pointed out the most acceptable—least distasteful?—way to achieve that independence. But could you rightly term it independence when the scheme, at its outset at least, required the charity of others?

Andrea sat a little longer, exhorting her flagging spirits into firm resolve. Then she jumped up and strode purposefully over to the dressing table and opened her small jewelry case. There was only one piece of any value in it. She lifted her mother's gold-chained pendant from its satin resting place.

The heart-shaped border of diamonds sprang to sparkling life in the sunshine streaming through the windows, the center ruby gleamed a rich blood-red. With it in her hand she hesitated a moment, trying not to think of the delight her mother must have felt on her sixteenth birthday when her father had clasped the necklace about her neck. Even Papa had not stooped so low as to "borrow" it to finance his gaming. Well, she could no longer indulge in sentimentality. Besides, she liked to believe that her mother, who had died when Andrea was only three, would be pleased to know that she was providing for her destitute daughter now. Andrea hesitated no longer. She wrapped the necklace carefully in a handkerchief and placed it inside her reticule.

She told no one but the parlormaid that she was going out, and wrapped in her heavy cloak, she stole furtively from the house, anxious to escape Emmy's questions and company. She was thankful for the icy air that pierced her lungs like needles and shocked her back to life. She hurried down the carriage drive, clutching her hood tightly around her face with one hand and holding the reticule, with its precious contents, with the other.

Under ordinary circumstances a walk from Kingswood to the village seemed a strenuous undertaking, rarely ventured upon as long as a carriage or donkey cart was available. Now Andrea was conscious neither of fatigue nor time. She climbed the rise that led to the small community, scarcely noticing the scattering of cottages on its outskirts. She passed the blacksmith's, the shoemaker's, the coaching inn, replying civilly to the greetings of folk she passed without really seeing them. When she reached her destination, she hesitated the merest moment, then resolutely opened the door and went inside.

Mr. Webster's shop was the village version of an Oriental bazaar, so varied was the merchandise he carried. It was a repository for cloth and bacon, shoes and tea, ribbons and ginger, buttons and flour; in short, for anything that Mr. Webster felt anyone might want at any moment.

There was only one customer in the shop, when Andrea entered, and Mr. Webster, glancing up, quickly summoned his twelve-year-old helper to wait on the farmer's wife while he wiped his hands on his apron and turned his beaming smile and personal attention toward this member of the upper class.

If Mr. Webster was surprised when Andrea murmured that she wished to speak to him in private, he showed no sign, of it. The merchant ushered her through a doorway into the tiny back room that had previously been his bachelor quarters but that he now shared with the nephew.

He still betrayed no surprise when Andrea explained what it was she wanted. His eyes did widen a bit, however, when she produced the jewelry and named the figure that she was asking for it.

Mr. Webster was a shrewd-enough businessman to realize that the amount was no more than half the jewel's worth; even so, it would strain his resources considerably to accommodate the young lady. Still, he had not been in business for twenty years without learning a thing or two. He was sure that he would shortly come up with a buyer. Instinctively, he opened his mouth to haggle over the price but then closed it. There was something in the set of Andrea's pale face that overrode his bargaining instincts. He paid her price and wished her a good day.

In spite of her long hike, Andrea was not ready to go back to the dower house and face the people there. It seemed a good time to take a look at the empty cottage her ladyship had spoken of.

She had no trouble finding the place, for it lay no more than a quarter-mile beyond the cottage that she and Emmy had visited the day before. She stood by the front gate and surveyed it with what she hoped was an objective eye.

It was larger than she'd expected, albeit tiny when compared to the prestigious school she and Emmy had attended. It had two stories. There were three small shuttered, square-paned windows symmetrically spaced across the top one, while on the lower floor there was a window on either side of a dark green door. The cottage itself appeared in good repair, although the surrounding garden was the victim of neglect. Andrea made her way down a weed-choked path and tried the door. It was unlocked. She stepped inside.

Again she was pleasantly surprised. The ground floor consisted of one single room with, luxury of luxuries, a fireplace at each end. She judged that it would easily accommodate twenty desks with room to spare for shelves. Now if only the first floor proved suitable for her living quarters.

She was halfway up the steep staircase when she heard a noise and froze. There was no time to be frightened before a running cloaked figure brushed past her, forcing her to clutch the railing to keep her footing. Andrea caught only a glimpse of the female whom she seemed to have flushed like a startled partridge and was left merely with a blurred impression of bright yellow hair escaping from the hood of a woven cloak pulled forward in a half-successful attempt to conceal a pretty face.

Andrea stood, transfixed, staring as the door slammed shut behind the woman, her heart still thumping wildly from the shock.

"Ahem." A throat was cleared above her, causing her to emit a choked-off screech and nearly lose her balance once again as she wheeled its way. She gazed upward into the amused eyes of Lord Blakeney.

Despite the chill that the thick walls could not shut out, he was in his shirtsleeves. He was, in fact, engaged in stuffing the tail of the garment into his riding breeches, an act that sent the blood rushing to Andrea's face. He grinned broadly at her embarrassment.

"Were you looking for me, Miss Prior?"

"Certainly not." She recovered quickly. Her voice was tart, a precursor, perhaps, of the schoolmistress she planned to become.

"Oh? And to what, then, do I owe the honor of this intrusion?"

"I had no notion that I would be intruding. When Lady Blakeney suggested that I look at this cottage, she assured me that it was unoccupied."

"It is. Except . . . occasionally," he drawled, folding his arms and leaning one shoulder against the wall. "But I'd no idea this was a showplace. Just why did my grandmother suggest you see it?"

"She had thought that I might be able to rent it from you to use as a schoolhouse. But I can see," she added dryly, "that you would be reluctant to part with it."

"For a school?" He looked astounded. "My grandmother is noted for her odd starts, but why, in God's name, a school?"

"Because I have my way to make and there aren't that many avenues open to women. Now, if you will excuse me—and accept my apologies for interrupting."

"That's nonsense." He ignored her attempt to terminate the conversation. "You'll take the avenue that most women take. You'll leg-shackle some poor, smitten male who will then take care of you."

"Oh, indeed? Without a dowry? How many ladies of your acquaintance have managed that?"

He shrugged. "I've really given the matter little thought. But it must happen now and then."

"So do meteors fall occasionally. But I would not waste my time expecting one to land in my front garden. But good day, sir. I'll let your grandmother know that this building wouldn't suit."

"No need to get on your high ropes. You're here. You might as well see the rest of the house."

"Another time, perhaps."

"Good lord! Don't tell me you're afraid of me, Miss Prior. I can assure you, I haven't dropped a frog down anyone's neck in donkey's years. See—nothing in my hands." He held them up, fingers spread, in mock innocence.

Well, why not? After all, she had come this far. She climbed the remaining stairs.

He stepped aside and, with a parody of a bow, gestured fulsomely at the door, which stood half open on the landing. She ignored his mischievous grin as she walked past him. But she was not quite so successful when it came to overlooking the dirty feather bed that occupied the center of an otherwise bare room.

She gazed about her with a pang for lost opportunities. Lady Blakeney was right. The cottage was perfect for her purposes. This floor was divided into two rooms. She crossed to look into the other. It was identical to the first except that the fireplace was in the opposite wall. What a wonderful parlor and bedchamber they could be.

She turned reluctantly from her examination of the second room and walked straight into the arms of Lord Blakeney. "Oh, come now, Miss Prior." He laughed as she struggled to free herself. "You must expect to pay a small forfeit for upsetting my morning's . . . agenda . . . the way you have." He cupped a hand beneath her chin and held it firmly as his lips found hers.

Andrea was conscious of two conflicting sensations: the shock of Blakeney's kiss, which was turning out to be teasing—almost tender, actually—instead of the lip-bruising assault she had expected; and the sound of heavy boots running up the stairs.

Blakeney seemed a bit slower than she had been to hear the footsteps, but he did manage to swing her around in time to face the door himself as it burst open. He released her slowly and she turned to see a young man poised upon the threshold, a riding whip gripped in a white-knuckled fist, his teeth bared, his face contorted.

"I dislike having to point this out, Zach," his lordship drawled, seeming not the least bit put out of countenance by the intrusion, "but in civil society it is customary to knock, you know."

Chapter
Six

The young man's expression had run the gamut from fury to astonishment, then back to sullen hatred. Andrea had no difficulty in placing him. He was the insolent fellow she and Emmy had seen coming out of Molly Cannon's cottage.

Lord Blakeney eyed the whip and chuckled. "Don't tell me that you, of all people, are playing knight-errant. Here to protect Miss Prior's virtue, are you? Well, I assure you, Galahad, it's quite unnecessary. Her virtue's safe with me."

The other man took a menacing step forward. Involuntarily, Andrea eased back. "Oh, her class protects her, does it?" he asked between clenched teeth.

"Well, no, if we must be so plainspoken. It's more her, er, unwillingness to cooperate. Perhaps 'virtue' is a better term."

"That's right," the young man sneered. "You can't force your droit du seigneur on a lady, can you, *your lordship*."

"Droit du seigneur!" Blakeney's laugh was genuine. "By gad, Zach, you do have some odd notions. I can assure you I've never forced my lordly rights on anyone. Nor has anybody else for centuries, I'll wager. No, I hate to pour cold water on your chivalrous notions, but I've never made love to anyone who wasn't more than willing. Well, ah"—he glanced sideways at Andrea—"present company excepted, of course. But then this wasn't what you might think. Not that I expect you to believe me."

"Actually, I do believe you. I don't think you're here on Miss Prior's account." Zach Cannon stared pointedly at the feather bed. "And I think you're damned lucky that I came too late."

"Are you threatening me, Zach?" Blakeney said softly. "All I can say is, it's midsummer's moon with you. We've been at daggers drawn all our lives and we've always found far better things to quarrel about than some doxy."

Zach's face contorted at the word and he took another step their way.

"Confess, man. Your *chivalry*," Blakeney mocked the word, "is just a pretense to cover your real quarrel with me. So, I suspect, is the way you've been stirring up my tenants. But that's considerably more serious, Zach. My tolerance is running out on that score."

"Your *tolerance*? What you really mean is that your *time* is running out." There was a fanatical gleam in the young man's eyes. "You and your kind are doomed and you damn well know it. The working people in this land will rise up and take back what's rightly theirs."

"So you keep on saying. How does your doggerel go?

"When Adam delved and Eve span,
Who was then the gentleman?"

"You can sneer now, m'lord." He turned the title into a profanity. "But you'll sing a different tune, I can assure you, when the downtrodden of this country claim back their own."

Neither of the men any longer seemed aware of Andrea's presence. She could have walked out of the room unnoticed, but she was incapable of such a sensible course of action.

"You'd really like that, wouldn't you, Zach? To see me all trussed up in a tumbril with you waiting there on the platform to personally drop the guil lotine blade. But as disappointing as the news will be to you, I have to inform you, it will never happen. This is England, man. Not some run-amok country like France. And while I'll grant you that there are plenty of wrongs that need to be righted, you should realize that things will be changed the English way, by law and not by revolution."

Blakeney's voice suddenly lost a bit of its belligerence and there was real concern in his voice. "It's your own neck you need to be concerned with, Zach. You're on a dangerous path. The penalties for treason aren't pretty."

"Tell that to the Americans. Or to the French."

Blakeney sighed. "You always were too hotheaded for your own good. And ready to set the Thames on fire. So go to the devil in your own way,

Zach, but leave my farm workers alone. Don't use them for your own personal vendetta. For you know as well as I do that there's no better housed and paid group of workers in the land. You persuade them to leave the fields and they'll be the losers, not me. Is that what you really want?"

"What I want is justice."

"Then you can whistle for it. For you're on the wrong road to find it."

"Am I?" the other asked softly. "Well, we'll see then, won't we?"

He wheeled abruptly and left the room. The sound of his boots could be heard clattering down the steps as swiftly as they'd come.

"Whooosh!" Andrea did not realize she'd been holding her breath until she suddenly released it.

Blakeney had been staring at the door, his expression unfathomable. Now he gave her a quizzical look. "Are you all right, Miss Prior?"

"Oh, yes. *I* am quite all right. But I collect that *you* owe me your heartfelt thanks."

"For one brief kiss? Oh, I think not. Especially since you quite failed to play your part in the exercise."

In the drama that had followed it, Andrea had managed to forget that particular exercise. She did not care to be reminded of it now.

"I was not referring to your breach of good manners, as you perfectly well know. That angry young man came here expecting to find you with the person who almost knocked me off the stairs in her haste to get away. She must have thought that I was he. Lucky for you that I decided to take a look at this house. Otherwise, he might have killed you."

"With a horse whip? Really, Miss Prior, you give

me very little credit. Now if he had brought a pistol, that might have been another matter entirely."

"Well, next time he might. Perhaps you should seriously consider renting out this house, Lord Blakeney. Good day, sir."

She walked swiftly to the door and then down the steps. As she closed the gate behind her, she looked back over her shoulder expecting that Lord Blakeney would follow. The cottage door remained firmly closed. And though she kept glancing back periodically until she reached the fork in the road that led to the manor house, he was not behind her. It occurred to her that the young woman with the yellow hair must have been lurking near the cottage all the time, waiting to resume their tryst. Andrea found this notion distasteful in the extreme.

As she opened the front door of the dower house, she was relieved to hear a male voice speaking in the withdrawing room. Her ladyship and Emmy were entertaining. That would at least postpone any awkward questions about where she had been all morning.

The reprieve was welcome. She longed for some moments alone to sort out the tangle of events she had just experienced. Had it only been a few hours since her father's letter had arrived? It seemed to her that there'd been drama enough in this day so far to fill an entire fortnight. She was moving quietly toward the stairs when Emmy called out, "Andrea, is that you?"

Suppressing a regretful sigh, Andrea acknowledged her presence.

"We have a guest. Do come and see who's here."

As she entered the withdrawing room, Mr. Beau Austen rose eagerly to his feet. He appeared most delighted to see her. It was impossible not to respond to his warm smile in kind.

She took a chair on the opposite side of a Pembroke table from Lady Blakeney, who poured her a steaming cup of tea. Mr. Austen and Emmy were sharing a sofa. Their empty cups indicated that he had been there for some time. "My host deserted me for some pressing estate business," he explained. "And my fellow guests were slugabeds. So I seized the opportunity to come calling on my own. Lady Blakeney has forgiven my effrontery."

Not even Lady Blakeney was immune to Mr. Austen's charm, it seemed. Her answering smile was warm, at least when measured by her usual standards. Andrea was surprised to find her first impressions of Mr. Austen validated. For she had decided, upon consideration, that she must have exaggerated his good looks and pleasing manner. Now she began to suspect that she had actually undervalued them.

"I fear I've been the bearer of ill tidings, though, Miss Prior. I told Blakeney of our chance meeting and broached the subject of the ball to him."

"And of course my odious cousin would not hear of it," Emmy interrupted in disgust. "Of all the shabby things. But then"—she brightened—"Mr. Austen came up with the most marvelous new scheme. And Grandmama has agreed. Oh, Andrea, you'll never guess it."

Fortunately, Andrea's psychic powers were not put to the test, for Emmy could not wait to share the news. "The thing is, we've decided to give a Valentine's party right here. Isn't it famous?"

Chapter Seven

The next few days were filled with preparations. And great excitement. At least on Emmy's part. Much thought was given to the guest list, "For we can't invite everyone we know to this dreary little house," she declared.

The guests from the Hall topped the list, of course. Then Emmy concentrated on choosing those of her neighbors most likely to appeal to the London gentlemen. Though not too much, Andrea thought privately, after two young ladies with some claim to beauty had been eliminated as "too tedious by half."

The last name on the list was a certain Miss Lucinda Sanders whom Emmy added from pure mischief. "She's had her cap set for Blake since she left the schoolroom and he can't abide her," she said, chuckling. "This will really make him cross as crabs."

"Emeline, you should be ashamed," Andrea scolded from her side of the library table where she had begun penning the cards of invitation to those guests whom her friend had definitely approved.

"Well, I'm not. Serves him right for not giving us a ball."

"But isn't that a bit hard on poor Miss Sanders?"

"Not in the least. She's too great a paperskull to notice the snubs. Besides, I hope she snares him. I'll certainly do my part by giving her the opportunity." She grinned wickedly as she underlined Miss Sanders's name for emphasis.

Although not nearly soon enough for Emmy, the evening of the party did at last arrive. After trying on every evening gown in her wardrobe and declaring each one "shockingly outmoded," Emmy finally settled on a round dress of Urling's net over pale pink satin, with the customary low neckline, high waist, and small puffed sleeves. The bottom of the skirt was trimmed with a deep lace flounce, which was festooned with bouquets of roses and bluebells. The same flowers encircled her hair, which had been pulled onto the crown of her head while a profusion of curls were left free to frame her face. Andrea thought her friend looked marvelous, if perhaps a trifle overdressed for a country party. By default, she herself settled on a simplified version of Emmy's gown, made of fine jaconet muslin with one unadorned ruffle of the same material to finish off the skirt.

The young gentlemen from the Hall had been asked to dinner before the other guests arrived. The three Londoners came suitably attired in dark tail-coats; white breeches, stockings, cravats, and collars; and black evening slippers. Lord Blakeney had chosen to appear instead in a gray tailcoat, fawn pantaloons, and hussar boots.

Emmy was incensed with her cousin. "Why can you never behave properly?" she hissed, supposedly for his ears alone while everyone else in the drawing room pretended not to hear. "Where are your evening clothes?"

"And where is your fichu?" he retorted. "Do you suppose our grandmother still owns something of the sort? That neckline of yours definitely needs filling in. Besides its questionable modesty, you're almost certain to take a chill." He grinned at her speaking look.

At dinner Emmy was strategically placed between Mr. Austen and Sir Nigel. That left Lord Blakeney, playing host for his grandmother, at the table's head, with Andrea on his left next to Lord Gresham. She considered her position to be the social equivalent of sailing between Scylla and Charybdis. But instinctively she chose to turn her back to Blakeney, rather pointedly, and talk instead to the other lord.

"I hope you're enjoying the hunting, Lord Gresham," she said politely after waiting a bit for a pause in the gentleman's food consumption. "We've heard the hounds out early every morning."

"Too damned early, if you ask me," he replied thickly through a mouthful of larded sweetbreads. He'd been eating greedily and noisily. His plate was overloaded, to the peril of the area around it.

"I suppose it must be the best time of day, however, to slaughter all of those harmless little creatures you gentlemen like to pursue." She smiled falsely.

There was a pause while his lordship washed down the sweetbreads with a huge gulp of claret. "They ain't harmless. Bunch of vermin actually. Foxes. Rabbits. But as for liking to pursue 'em, never did. That's what you have gamekeepers for, to cull out all the pests."

"If you don't care for hunting, I'm surprised you came. I had been led to understand that that was the purpose of your visit."

"Well, I had to get out of town, didn't I? Me wife's due to foal at any minute."

Andrea gaped at him. "Are you saying that your wife is about to give birth, sir?" Her astonishment was rapidly giving way to indignation.

"That's right." He helped himself to macaroni as a footman sprang forward to refill his wineglass. "Didn't know I was leg-shackled, eh? Someone should have told you. Waste of your time casting your lures out at me."

The sound of a chuckle from Lord Blakeney's direction did little to cool Andrea's rising temper. "I neither know nor care about your marital status, Lord Gresham. But I admit that I'm astounded that you should wish to leave your wife at such a time."

For the first time his lordship shifted his gaze from his plate to look straight at her. "Best time in the world to get away, I'd call it. All that fuss and feathers. Leave it to the females. It's nothing to say to me." He suddenly grinned lasciviously. "Did me part in the thing nine months ago, now, didn't I?" He winked and redirected his attention to his plate.

Andrea turned away in disgust to meet the

amused gaze of Blakeney. "Charming friends you have," she commented under her breath.

"Never saw him in my life before he came here," he murmured back. "He's the Beau's friend, not mine."

"Well, I am astonished."

"Thought you might be."

As they left the dining chamber, the party guests were beginning to arrive. Andrea had no difficulty in picking out Miss Sanders from among the throng of eager young people. Recognition was not so much due to Emmy's unflattering description as to the fact that one young woman immediately left the ladies with whom she'd been conversing to elbow through the crowd and attach herself to Lord Blakeney. Andrea had some difficulty in smothering a smile at the look of distaste that briefly crossed his face.

The unfortunate young lady clearly suffered by comparison to the yellow-haired, lowborn beauty Andrea had glimpsed upon the cottage stairway. The heiress's face was long and narrow, with teeth to match. Her laugh, which sounded across the room as she greeted Blakeney, had a slight whinnying quality in keeping with the rest of her appearance. All in all, she seemed exactly the sort of female one might wish upon Lord Blakeney.

The odd thing was, though, that for once Andrea could see why the heiress just might be attracted by something other than an ancient title and estate. If one did not know Blakeney quite so well, one might consider him distinguished-looking, perhaps even handsome. His physique certainly passed muster, with its broad shoulders, narrow waist, and well-shaped legs. And his eyes . . . Fortunately,

Emmy's preemptive hand clapping brought an end to this unproductive train of thought.

"May I have your attention?" the petite hostess called, and the babble of voices that had filled the withdrawing room obligingly ceased. "Since this *is* a Valentine's party," Emmy informed them, "I am about to revive an old, old custom, which goes back, some folk believe, all the way to the Romans. Samuel!" she called to a footman who was standing by. "You may bring the urn in now."

The servant vanished and reappeared shortly bearing an enormous Chinese porcelain jar, which he set on the floor in front of his mistress. "What we have here is a magical urn," she announced solemnly, although her eyes were laughing, "such as might have been found in Aladdin's cave."

"Aren't you getting your periods a bit mixed, Emmy?" her cousin inquired dampeningly. "What happened to the Romans?"

"Well, never mind where the custom came from. The point is, our futures are ready to unfold. For inside this jar are twenty hearts, each bearing the name of a young lady in our company."

This announcement was met with a series of anticipatory titters.

"And you gentlemen are to each draw one from the jar and pin it to your sleeve. What's more, you must wear it until February fourteenth, thereby announcing to all and sundry that the young lady whose name you wear is, indeed, your true valentine."

The giggles increased in intensity while the young men gave one another sheepish looks. "And," Emmy ended on a more practical note, "the same young lady will also be your partner for supper. All right then, Blakeney, you begin."

Lord Blakeney's look was withering. "Emmy, when it comes to jingle-brained ideas, you have no peers. But, by Jove, you've topped yourself. If you think I'm going to go about with a stupid paper heart pinned on my sleeve, you've maggots on the brain. No thank you."

This dampening declaration had no chance to cast a pall. Mr. Austen stepped quickly into the breach. "Here, let *me* be first then. I can hardly wait to seal my fate." And he fished eagerly in the jar.

Afterward Andrea was to question the coincidence. For the red heart he came up with and waved triumphantly in the air bore the name of none other than his hostess.

The rush to the jar was on. Mr. Austen seemed to have struck the proper note, for if any gentleman present was disappointed in his valentine, you would not have guessed it. There was much laughing and joking and clapping of hands as name after name was drawn. Sir Nigel drew a sweet-faced miss who proved to be the vicar's second daughter. Andrea held her breath as Lord Gresham fished in the jar. To her immense relief he did not draw her name but that of an unlucky neighbor. All of the hearts were rapidly being pinned upon the sleeves of long-tailed evening coats before Andrea woke up to the realization that her own had not been drawn. Thanks to the churlish Lord Blakeney, her valentine was languishing in the Chinese jar. Andrea could not help but wonder if this was not, indeed, a portent of things to come.

Card tables had been set up in the smaller drawing room and dancing was to take place in the larger. Andrea was glad that she had volunteered to play the pianoforte since by common consent the couples were pairing off according to the valentine lottery. At least her partnerless state would not be quite so obvious.

She was not forgotten, though. After the first set Mr. Austen appeared at her side, volunteering to turn the sheet-music pages. "But you'll be needed for dancing," she protested.

"No, I won't." He pulled a chair close beside her. "Miss Sedley has made sure that Blake takes a turn." He nodded toward the floor where the dancers were taking their places for the cotillion. Sure enough, a wooden-faced Lord Blakeney was standing beside Miss Sanders. Andrea giggled before she thought and Mr. Austen broke into a wide grin. "Serves him right for shirking the valentine drawing."

"Oh, well. As for that, I can only applaud his churlishness."

"Because your name was the one left in the jar? Well, the more fool he. I only wish I'd had his chance." His eyes were intense as they gazed into hers.

Andrea was hard-pressed to maintain her composure. His words, his gaze, and most of all his nearness were most unsettling.

"Oh, come now, Mr. Austen, I am certain that you somehow contrived to draw Emmy's name."

"Now how could I have possibly done so?" he protested. "I assure you, if there were any contriving to be done . . . Oh, not that I don't find Miss Sedley utterly charming, but *she* is not the most beautiful young lady in the room."

"We're waiting, Andrea dear." There was the merest tinge of asperity in Emmy's voice as she called from her position beside Sir Nigel. Everyone was looking at the musician expectantly. Andrea began to play, quite loudly in order to discourage any further uncomfortable conversation.

But as Mr. Austen also refocused his attention on the music, he seemed to find it necessary to keep his face quite close to her own and breathe into her ear as he turned the pages. He performed this duty superbly. Andrea's fingers were never forced to falter between bars. "Thank you," she said primly at the dance's conclusion, trying to erect a barrier of formality between them after the intimacy of the past several minutes.

"It was my pleasure." He aped her proper tone, then smiled engagingly. "We make an excellent team, do we not, Miss Prior?"

"No doubt." A dry voice spoke behind them. "But you'll have to harness yourself to another filly for a bit, Beau. My cousin's waiting. For you, I believe. I'll take care of the page turning."

Lord Blakeney sank gratefully into the chair that his friend had vacated and stretched out his legs. "Thank God, that's done," he muttered.

"Oh? You don't care for dancing then?"

"Under some circumstances." He stared glumly at the dance floor, where the young people were changing partners.

Andrea, though she had resolved not to, watched Mr. Austen make his bow to Emmy and took note of the warm smile he gave her. His charm seemed undiminished. It played no favorites. She wondered what her friend would think if she had overheard the intimate conversation at the piano. Well, she would never disclose it. Her lips were sealed.

"I hope you and Emmy aren't going to get into a hair-pulling over the Beau."

Lord Blakeney appeared to have acquired the

knack of reading minds. Andrea turned a frosty look his way. "I beg you pardon?"

"You heard me. Dropping an accomplished flirt down between a couple of green 'uns like you and my cousin really is setting the cat among the pigeons. I've always known that Emmy's not possessed of any common sense. But I'd like to believe that you have enough wit not to spoil a lifelong friendship."

"I'm truly touched by your concern." Her voice was laden with heavy sarcasm. "I know how much you've always valued my and Emeline's attachment."

He shrugged. "You're right. It's nothing to me. Except that I'd hate to add two more feuding females into the Kingswood mix."

"You may rest assured, your lordship, that Emmy and I will not disturb your peace."

For the second time the musician had to be prompted to begin. But once started, the music, lively and spirited, showing off the performer's considerable skill, fairly propelled the dancers by its own momentum. Till suddenly it faltered to a halt.

"Turn!" she hissed.

Lord Blakeney snapped to and obligingly turned the page.

"If you're going to do this, pray pay attention," she said between clenched teeth as her fingers once more flew.

"No point in that. Can't read a note of music."

"Then just what are you doing here?"

"Getting away from the cursed dancing, what else?" He leaned over and flipped the page, sixteen bars too soon, throwing the country dance into mass confusion.

Chapter Eight

"**I** *am sure you must be tired, Miss Prior.*" Miss Sanders wore a determined look as she stood by the pianoforte. "I shall be happy to play a while."

Andrea thanked her gratefully and relinquished her seat. "You'll find Lord Blakeney a most able assistant," she added mischievously, carefully averting her eyes from that gentleman. "My playing would not have been the same without him."

"Ah, but you surely cannot have forgotten, Miss Prior, that you and I are engaged for your first dance. I know Miss Sanders will excuse us since this is your opportunity to join in the evening's fun."

As she watched Miss Sanders's face fall, Andrea could cheerfully have kicked her unwelcome partner. But before they could take the floor, Emmy intercepted them and grasped her cousin's arm.

"Blakeney," she hissed, "you must do something about your odious friend."

"Oh? And what has Beau done now, pray tell?"

"I don't mean Mr. Austen, as you know perfectly well. I'm referring to your loathsome Lord Gresham."

"He's not *my* Lord Gresham, but never mind that. Just tell me the problem."

"He's at the loo table. Everyone there had expected to play for fish and he's insisted on high stakes. Joe Thatcher has lost almost all of his next quarter's allowance and poor Miss Rutledge is on the verge of tears. I want you to put an immediate stop to it!"

"Oh, God, why me? This is your cursed party." Nonetheless, he strode off toward the game room.

After that Banbury tale he had spun for Miss Sanders's benefit, he could at least have apologized for abandoning me, Andrea fumed silently.

Sir Nigel was coming their way, however. She suspected that Emmy was his intended target, but that young lady's hand was claimed moments before he reached them. If he had, indeed, been disappointed, it did not show. Sir Nigel's bow and smile were unexceptional as he invited Andrea to dance. She accepted gladly, neither knowing nor caring whether she was second choice.

After she had broken through his initial shyness, Sir Nigel proved to be delightful company, possessed of a ready wit. His stammer went away, she noticed, as he grew less self-conscious. If he had a fault as a dance partner, it was that his eyes seemed to be straying toward Emmy more often than was flattering. But since she was prone to gaze in the same direction for the pleasure of watching Mr.

Austen's skill in dancing, she could not be too censorious of this social lapse.

Once Mr. Austen seemed aware of her eyes upon him and flashed her a brilliant smile over his partner's head. She felt her face grow warm and was careful not to glance his way again.

The party was undoubtedly a huge success. The dancing had continued to the point of exhaustion with no young lady left to languish without a partner for any length of time. The high-stakes loo game had been replaced by a noisy game of lottery tickets to everyone's relief, with the possible exception of Lord Gresham. And no one really cared for his opinion.

Supper, served at midnight, took them by surprise, the guests all declaring that they'd no idea it could possibly be so late. The evening had certainly flown. All of the young gentlemen joined the young ladies whose hearts they wore and escorted them into the dining chamber. Andrea tried to appear absorbed in sorting out the sheet music on the pianoforte to cover her embarrassment at being the single unattached female in the company. She was aware of Lord Blakeney watching her activity from across the room and longed to wipe the amused look off his face. He took his own good time before sauntering toward her.

"It seems we're the only two left, Miss Prior."

"That's because you refused to take part in Emmy's game."

"Would you really have wanted me to go around for days with a silly paper heart with your name on it pinned to my sleeve?"

"Most certainly not."

"Well, there you are then." He offered her his

arm. Her fingers made minimum contact with the gray superfine.

To her disappointment, they did not join the lively group gathered around Emmy and Mr. Austen. Instead, he placed chairs for them in an isolated corner, then went to fill their plates from the cold collation that overwhelmed the dining table. She watched with envy the laughing faces turned toward Mr. Austen as he told some anecdote. Miss Sanders, she noted, was among that group. This no doubt accounted for her own isolation.

Lord Blakeney obviously did not equate females with dainty appetites. He returned with two heaped-up plates and sat down beside her. "Have you known Sir Nigel and Mr. Austen long?" she inquired with formal politeness as they began to eat.

He waited to swallow a mouthful of ham. "How long have I known Beau?" he rephrased her question. "Since about age nine, I'd say. Why?"

"Because, one, one has to converse about something, and, two, he seems an odd choice of friend for you."

"Because he deals in Spanish coin and I don't? Having a different viewpoint where females are concerned doesn't affect our friendship."

"I have noticed the difference," she replied acidly. "Which reminds me. I have wanted to ask about the man who came to your, ah, young woman's rescue."

"Rescue?" His eyebrows shot up. "I can assure you that if anybody needs rescuing in that situation it isn't—but never mind. The name is really none of your affair."

"My interest was in the *man* and not your con-

72

quests," she retorted with considerable heat. "He clearly is not one of your admirers."

"That's the understatement of all understatements. To put it in a nutshell, he hates me."

"Why?"

He gave the matter some thought. "Because he would like to be me."

Andrea laughed, a bit derisively. "You do have a high opinion of yourself, Lord Blakeney. What you most likely mean is that he would like to have what you have."

"Amounts to the same thing, doesn't it?"

"I do not think so. With people like Orator Hunt and others of the same persuasion, it is not a personal matter. They simply wish to see a more equitable distribution of the world's goods. Or so I understand."

"Well, I can assure you that no matter what political cant Zach Cannon may spout, with him it *is* entirely personal. We've been at each other's throats, quite literally, since we first got out of leading strings. He gave me this"—he tapped the tiny scar that ran down his cheek to his upper lip—"when we were eleven or so. Threw a rock. Of course," he added, grinning, "I was chasing him on horseback at the time."

"What a despicable thing to do!"

"Oh, I had no real intention of running him down. He, on the other hand, clearly meant to knock me off my horse. I obliged him by jumping off and drawing his claret with a facer." He chuckled at the memory. "It was quite a bloody row."

"Lord Blakeney, I'd thank you to mind your tongue."

"Miss Prior, pull your own mind up from the gut-

73

ter. It was a bloody row literally, not profanely."
He gave her a hard look. "You really don't think
much of me, do you?"

"What I think of you—or you of me, when it comes
to that—is not of the slightest consequence and
should not affect our business dealings in the least."

"We have business dealings?" He appeared genuinely surprised. "Oh, I see. You're referring to the
cottage." He paused to spear and eat a potted
shrimp. "You did say something about wanting to
start a school there, didn't you? But I supposed it
was just a harebrained notion of the moment that
you would soon forget."

"It was nothing of the kind. As I explained, I have
my own way to make."

"Even so, I can't picture you as a schoolmistress."

"Oh, no? Then just how do you picture me, Lord
Blakeney?"

His eyes lit up with mischief. His grin barely
missed being lecherous. "Oh, I don't think you really want me to answer that, Miss Prior."

It was just as well that the party began to break
up at that point. For Andrea was at a loss to come
up with a retort that would be scathing enough by
half.

Chapter Nine

"*I know a spot where we are almost certain to get a good view of the hunt.*"

Emmy's eyes shone at the prospect. Andrea was a great deal less enthusiastic about venturing forth on a bone-chillingly damp morning for the dubious pleasure of seeing a group of men on horseback pursue a small fox, already harried by a pack of hounds. But for her friend's sake, she kept her reservations to herself.

The hunt had been planned at the Valentine's party, the young men from the neighborhood insisting that courtesy demanded that the London gentlemen get a true taste of the shire's sport. Lord Blakeney had succumbed to pressure. He had held firm, however, when his cousin Emmy suggested that ladies be allowed to take part in the fun.

"I make it a rule never to hunt with females. You

spend half your time scooping them up off the ground after they've slipped off those cursed side-saddles. It always happens just when the action gets going."

"That's not true," his cousin retorted. "I'm a good rider and you know it."

"You're a complete incompetent," he said witheringly, and the discussion was closed.

For once Andrea was in accord with Lord Blakeney, if not for the same reasons. Like Emmy, she considered herself a good rider, but she had no desire to join in the hunt. Her sympathies in that exercise were entirely with the fox.

She did not even wish to see the poor thing pursued and was about to beg off. But then she recognized the fact that the hunt itself was of small importance. It was Mr. Austen that Emmy really wished to see, not a harried animal. And the least she could do, as friend and guest, was to bear her company. The fact that she, too, was not averse to seeing Mr. Austen was a point she didn't dwell on.

As they trudged up the hill that Emmy promised was bound to overlook the hunt at one stage or another, they could hear the hounds baying in the distance. The sun shone sickly just above a distant wood as if it, like Andrea, had been loath to rise. The wind picked up when they reached the unprotected summit. They pulled their woolen cloaks tightly around themselves and stamped their half boots on the frozen ground to warm their icy feet.

Fortunately, they hadn't long to wait before the dog pack broke out of the trees, sniffing the cleared ground excitedly. They were soon followed by a dozen or so men on horseback.

Andrea was forced to admit to herself that the

hunt did make a splendid spectacle, with the riders dressed in their bright pink coats, mounted on their magnificent animals, and galloping headlong down the valley in hot pursuit of the hounds.

At least one of the gentlemen spied them on their hillside vantage point. He detached himself from the group and rode their way.

"Oh, Mr. Austen, you should not have left the hunt on our account." Emmy's smile of pleasure belied her words as Beau Austen lifted his hat in greeting. "If you don't hurry, you'll miss all the fun."

"Not a bit of it. In fact, seeing you young ladies is the high point of my day. I know I shall sink myself below reproach by admitting it, but I've little enthusiasm for fox hunting."

His smile, which encompassed both young ladies equally, made it quite evident that he suffered little anxiety over falling out of favor. Andrea certainly liked him better for his frank admission.

"Tell me," Emmy asked curiously, "who was that riding Horatio? It looked too bulky to be my cousin. But still, I cannot imagine Blake permitting anyone else to ride him."

"You are right. On both counts. Lord Gresham insisted on riding Horatio. Said that none of the other horses were up to his weight. He may have had a point. I wouldn't know. I can't report that Blake gave in to his demands with a very good grace, but he did give in. Finally."

"I can hardly believe it. Blake idolizes that animal. I cannot imagine his ever letting anyone else mount Horatio."

"Well, as I said, he didn't do it gladly." Mr. Austen chuckled at the memory. "But hostly duty did

77

at last prevail. And speaking of painful duty, I shall have to rejoin the pack or be sent to Coventry." He gave the ladies a last, regretful bow and then galloped off after the disappearing hunt.

The young ladies stood their ground a little longer, flailing themselves with their arms in an attempt to keep the blood circulating while they listened to the fading baying and the diminishing hoofbeats. "We'll freeze if we don't keep moving," Emmy declared between chattering teeth. "Let's go on down the valley after them. At least we'll be more sheltered from the wind."

They had trudged about a mile farther on when Andrea suggested it would be wise to head back to the dower house while they still had the strength to make it.

"It's already too late," Emmy said, turning toward a low stone wall that enclosed an orchard. "I'm exhausted. Let's rest a bit. Then we can go home if you wish it."

They settled gratefully on the wall while Emmy gave it as her opinion that the hunt might very well double back in their direction.

"If so," Andrea replied, "our best vantage point is still on the hilltop. Maybe they'll be so obliging as to come back just as we reach it."

"Like a staged spectacle, you mean?" Emmy laughed. "And us with a first-row balcony seat—oh, my goodness, listen!"

The baying of the hounds had picked up, both in excitement and volume.

"What did I tell you? They're headed back this way."

And as if on cue a furry red streak burst out of the orchard and leaped the wall between them.

"Run!"

The warning was unnecessary. Emmy had already hiked up her skirts and was racing across the open field toward a clump of trees. Andrea streaked after her.

They sheltered behind two oaks just in time to peer around the trunks as the leader of the dog pack sailed over the wall. The others, in full cry, came after him.

A hunting horn blared as the horsemen zigzagged their way into the orchard. Lord Blakeney, riding a large roan, was the first to break out of the trees, take the stone wall neck or nothing, and go tearing across the clearing after the hounds. The other members of the hunt were not far behind. Their horses jumped the wall without difficulty and set off in hot pursuit.

Andrea was intent on the chase, now progressing back up the valley, when she heard a bellow, then a crash, then a horse's terrified whinnying and a stream of curses. She jerked around to see Lord Gresham's mount thrashing on the ground while he, swearing like a trooper, extracted a boot that was tangled in the stirrup and crawled away.

The two girls raced toward the accident scene, oblivious to any danger from stragglers yet to come. Beau Austen, the last rider in the hunt, sailed easily over the wall, saw the accident, and dismounted just as the girls arrived upon the scene. The vanguard horsemen, hearing the cries of the downed animal as it struggled desperately to rise, abandoned the fox and the hounds and headed back one by one.

Sickened by the fear and suffering in the poor beast's eyes, Andrea was forced to turn away. Lord

Gresham had lumbered to his feet and was taking an exploratory step or two. He glanced her way and misinterpreted her white face and the tears gathering in her eyes. "There, there, young lady." He patted her shoulder awkwardly. "There's no need to take on so. I assure you, I'm quite all right."

"*You're* all right!" A rough hand grabbed his upper arm and jerked him around. Lord Blakeney was breathing fire. "You damned, cow-handed cawker, you've broken Horatio's leg!"

"Now see here! No need to take that tone," Gresham sputtered. "Could've happened to anyone. The damn fool horse wouldn't obey me. You should school your cattle better, Blakeney."

"Why, you lobcock bas—"

Sir Nigel quickly thrust himself in front of Blakeney and grabbed his threatening arm. "Easy, old man," he said soothingly. "Know how you must feel, but there's nothing to be gained by drawing his claret."

"Just let him try it," Gresham blustered. "By God, he's not man enough!" He failed to put up a struggle, though, as Beau Austen led him away.

"Let's go," Emmy whispered.

With a last look at the horse, lying still now as a white-faced, teary-eyed Blakeney knelt beside him stroking his neck and whispering soothingly, Andrea turned away. Emmy hurried to Mr. Austen's mount, which had wandered off and was nibbling at a clump of dried-up grass, and took it by the bridle. Andrea followed her reluctantly back toward the grove of trees where Mr. Austen was earnestly trying to calm Lord Gresham. She had no desire to be in that odious gentleman's company.

Once there she forced herself to turn again toward the tragic tableau. Blakeney was waving the others away. He took the pistol that a shaken groom was holding and placed it against the horse's head. Andrea covered her face with her hands. The report seemed to echo through the valley endlessly.

"My God! The bedlamite shot the curst animal himself!" Lord Gresham exclaimed with deep disgust. "What's he got grooms for, now, I ask you?"

"Oh, do be quiet!" Emmy snapped.

Andrea felt tears running between her fingers.

Chapter Ten

Andrea did wish that Emmy would change the subject. They were seated in the small withdrawing room sharing a worktable. Emmy had gone on and on about the accident. Andrea, on the other hand, had tried unsuccessfully for the past twenty-four hours to get it out of her head. She kept seeing that magnificent animal, bewildered and suffering, thrashing to get up. Nor could she erase the memory of the agonized look on Blakeney's face as he held the pistol to the creature's head.

"Sir Nigel said that Lord Gresham was completely to blame." Emmy looked with some dissatisfaction at her stitches but abandoned any notion of redoing them. "That he had no business being on Horatio in the first place. He said a plodding cob would have been more the thing." She giggled. "For once I was in complete sympathy with Blakeney."

"Well, thank you, cousin."

Both young ladies jumped at the voice from the doorway. "Do you have to sneak up on us that way," Emmy protested, sucking her injured thumb. "You've made me jab a needle into myself."

"Clumsy. And I didn't *sneak* in. I walked. Normally. If you hadn't been so busy gossiping, you'd have heard me. Where's Grandmama?" He came into the room and both young ladies gasped.

Lord Blakeney, though less carelessly dressed than usual in a riding coat, top boots, and an artfully arranged cravat, had a decidedly battered appearance. One eye was nearly swollen shut and there was an ugly bruise on his lower jaw.

"Blake, you've been fighting!" Emmy exclaimed.

"How very astute you are." He grinned sarcastically, then winced at its effect on a split lip. "Always sharp as a pin, eh, Emmy?"

"And you got much the worst of the brawl evidently."

"Not a bit of it. You should see the other cove."

"Then you did thrash that odious Lord Gresham. Well, as I was remarking, I can't say that I blame you. After what he did to Horatio."

"Stow it, Emmy." Lord Blakeney was obviously not ready to discuss the tragic accident. "And of course I didn't thrash Gresham, though I will admit that the notion's appealing. But it wouldn't be the thing. He is a guest under my own roof, more's the pity.

"By the by"—he turned an enigmatic look toward Andrea—"he tells me that you were the only person sympathetic to his part in the thing."

She looked astonished. And then indignant. "He actually said that? Why, of all the out-and-out bouncers! How ever could he have come up with such a harebrained notion?"

"He said you cried over him."

"Over him? Over *him*! Why, that bumptious cox-comb! I was crying for the *horse*." (And perhaps a bit for you, she might have added.)

"I see." His lordship's expression still did not give much away. "Well, I collect he actually believes his version. I suppose he has a need to think that some-one was sympathetic. He got short shrift at the Hall."

"But you didn't fight with him?" Emmy refused to be diverted.

"Of course not. You don't think that hen-hearted milksop could land me a facer, do you?"

"At least *two* facers," his cousin corrected. "But if not him, then who?"

"None of your affair, coz."

"Oh!" The insightful exclamation was out before Andrea could stop it. It earned her a repressive look from his lordship.

"Some cuckolded husband caught up with you then?" Emmy chuckled. "Serves you right."

"You do have a low mind, dear little cousin. I never get involved with married types."

"Never?" Emmy looked skeptical.

"Never. Now where's Grandmama?"

"In the library. But this is not a good time to see her. She's been a regular bear all morning. I'd leave her alone if I were you."

"I'd be more than happy to oblige. But, unfortu-nately, she sent for me. Ladies." He made an ex-aggerated leg and left them.

"What do you suppose?" Emmy whispered. "I'll wager Grandmama's got wind of his fight and is about to rake him over the coals about it. I can't wait to discover who he's been brawling with. Come on."

As she rose to follow Emmy, Andrea's conscience

was telling her that this was not at all the sort of conduct she should be engaged in. But curiosity gained the upper hand. Emmy turned and put a warning finger to her lips as they approached the library. The door was slightly ajar. They eased within earshot.

Eavesdropping was not difficult. Lady Blakeney's voice was raised in anger. "I want that rascal thrown off the estate, Blakeney. Immediately. Do you hear me?"

"Without the slightest difficulty, ma'am. I'll be amazed if they don't hear you at the Hall."

"None of your impudence, sir! I repeat, I want him off the property."

"I don't like to have to say this, Grandmama"—Blakeney's voice was surprisingly gentle—"but it is my property. And I'm not going to throw Zach off it. He has a right here, you know."

"A right?" she sneered. "You sound like a cursed Jacobin yourself."

"Hardly. But I will go down that road far enough to say that his people have worked our land as far back, I collect, as we've held it, which gives him some claim. This is his home, too."

"He forfeits all right to call it so when he begins to agitate our workers against us."

"If that's what's disturbing you, ma'am, forget it. He's having very little success with his agitation."

"So *you* say. Samuel tells me there's talk of not planting the spring crops."

"And that's all it is, talk. Oh, I don't doubt that a few hotheads or shiftless types may let Zach persuade them to bite off their noses to spite their faces. But the majority of our people aren't going to take the bread out of their own children's mouths. They have decent working conditions here and they know it."

"The best in England." The dowager sniffed. "But that won't stop the radicals. They'd pull the country down around their ears as long as they could take our kind with it. That is the way Zachery Cannon feels. Do you deny it?"

"No."

"Then get rid of him."

"No."

There was a long silence. The eavesdroppers looked at each other, wide-eyed. They could imagine grandmother and grandson glaring at each other.

"You are a fool then."

"Perhaps." He sighed. "But look at the other side of things. Kingswood is the best place for him to be right now. I don't think he'll do us much harm. And, firebrand that he is, he could land in serious trouble anywhere else."

"That is his lookout."

"Mostly, I'll grant you. But we have some obligation. Noblesse oblige, you know."

"Fustian!"

He laughed. "All right then. That is doing it a bit brown. But the man does have legitimate grievances."

"Indeed he has not." The girls flinched as her ladyship's stick struck the floor for emphasis. "He has been treated better than any other tenant on the estate. Which, if you ask me, is his trouble. Ideas above his station. He has no grievances. How dare you!"

"No need to fly off into the boughs, ma'am. I was speaking of grievances against the government, not us. Don't forget he fought for king and country. Zach Cannon survived Waterloo, only to be turned out of the army along with a quarter million other

86

men without any pension or any provision for making their way in civilian life. It's small wonder that they're talking sedition."

"That is as may be. And it is the government's problem. Our responsibility is to Kingswood. And I tell you that Zachery Cannon will not stop until he ruins you, Blakeney. He has hated you from the time you both learned to walk. You have brawled your whole lives. And now look at you. You are still at it. What effect do you think that will have on our people? Lord Blakeney, actually fistfighting with a member of the lower classes. Have you stopped to consider how it undermines your authority, sir?"

"Oh, I don't think so, ma'am." There was a low chuckle. "At least not so long as I get the best of it."

A slight movement from Emmy caused Andrea to glance her way. Her face was contorted in the beginning of a sneeze. She had pressed a finger under her nose. "Move!" Andrea mouthed, setting the example by tiptoeing rapidly away from the doorway, her soft-soled shoes making almost no sound in the marble hall.

"Ker-choo!"

Emmy had somehow managed to reach the sanctuary of the drawing room before the sneeze exploded.

Both girls collapsed on the settee in a fit of nervous laughter. Lady Blakeney's majordomo, finding them in this state, did not bother to hide his disapproval at such undignified conduct. "Lord Gresham is calling," he announced.

His lordship, following closely behind, took an entirely different view. "Well, I must say," he said as he strode into the room and sat, uninvited, in the largest available chair, "it is nice to be somewhere cheerful for a change. It's like a wake up at the Hall. Everybody Friday-faced and looking at me like I was some kind of criminal. And all over a curst horse. They'd be a lot less bothered if it had been me that got a broken leg, I can assure you."

"I expect you're right." Emmy gave him a hostile look. "For *you* would not have had to be shot."

Gresham appeared not to have heard and continued in the same aggrieved tone. "Even offered to pay for the beast, don't you know. And I will say this much for Blakeney, he refused to take me blunt. And only proper, by God. For if he'd schooled his precious cattle properly they'd know how to take a fence."

Andrea was relieved when a tea tray was brought in, creating a distraction. Emmy and her cousin might not share much affection for each other, but a love of horseflesh seemed to be in the Blakeney blood. The business of pouring preempted any retort she might have made.

"Do you live in London year-round, Lord Gresham?"

Even to Andrea's own ears this seemed a feeble attempt at a subject change, but it was the best she could come up with.

"Good lord, no." Gresham looked astounded at the question. "Nobody lives in London all year round. Got houses in York and Lancaster. Always stay in the metropolis for the Season, though. Wouldn't have left this time except to escape the lying-in."

They paused in their tea drinking at the sound of the library door being closed. Lord Blakeney's face was carefully blank as his eyes flickered over the scene. "Regular little tea party, I see."

"Yes. Please do join us."

The fact that the invitation smacked of sincerity was an indication of just how tedious Emmy was finding Lord Gresham's company.

"No thank you. Must have a word with my bailiff."

Gresham had actually paused in his voracious consumption of seedcake to stare at his host's battered face. "My word, Blakeney, what happened to you?"

"Sleepwalking," Lord Blakeney prevaricated without even an eye blink. "Got up in the wee hours of the night and walked smack into a door."

"Humph!" Lord Gresham's exclamation was eloquent of disbelief.

"I'll see you out," Emmy volunteered, and her cousin's eyebrows rose.

"If you're about to ask for an advance on your allowance, I'll save you the exercise. The answer is no."

"Oh, for heaven's sake! Can't one do the polite without your jumping to all sorts of stupid conclusions?"

Emmy flounced out of the room at Blakeney's side, and Lord Gresham, much to Andrea's discomfort, seized the opportunity to take the seat she had vacated. His small eyes bored into hers with what he seemed to intend as a look of sympathy.

"Damned shame about you having to rusticate here, Miss Prior."

"Oh, not at all, Lord Gresham." She tried not to make it obvious as she inched away from the pressure of his thigh, which was bulging in his modishly tight pantaloons. It was inevitable, she supposed, that a man of his size would take up most of the settee; even so, such close proximity was distasteful. "Miss Sedley and I have been friends since our infancy," she elaborated. "I've spent many happy visits here with her. I enjoy them above all things."

"Still, it's a damn shame. Heard about your father, don't you know. Had no business playing deep when he's got a daughter to see to." The porcine face endeavored to look virtuous. "Handsome gel like you shouldn't be stuck in this backwater. Should be in London. At Almack's. You'd put all those mamas with their antidotes of daughters into a real taking." He chuckled. "Your beauty against their fortunes. That would certainly put all the single coves in a pucker."

"Not really," Andrea said dryly. "I'm sure that fortune would be victorious every time."

He took a moment to think the matter over. "You're right, I collect. A man has to look after his best interests when it comes to getting leg-shackled. My wife had a damned fine dowry. Would have had to have had. She's one of those antidotes I mentioned."

"Lord Gresham, I do not think it at all proper for—"

"What you need," he continued thoughtfully as he reached over to pat her hand, almost absent-mindedly, "is someone to look after you. A sort of patron, don't you know."

"Indeed I do know," she replied frostily, withdrawing her hand to pick up her teacup. "And I can assure you that I have one. I call him Papa."

To her immense relief, Emmy came back into the room and put a period to the distasteful tête-à-tête.

Chapter
Eleven

"*Surely you must be funning!*"

"I could not be more serious. We agreed, did we not, to try out all the old Valentine's customs?"

The young ladies had been served their morning cups of tea in bed and were sipping them while the newly revived fire was heating up their bedchamber. Emmy had proposed her latest scheme.

"But midnight!" Andrea protested.

"I realize that it's inconvenient. But there's always something magical about midnight, don't you know."

"In February there's always something frigid about midnight. Besides, what will your grandmother say?"

"She's not to know, is she? Oh, come now, Andrea, don't be such a damper. You did agree to try everything, remember?"

"Well, yes," Andrea admitted. "But this one is so absurd. Sillier even than eggs and laurel leaves."

"It is not. It's really the most likely of all the charms to get results."

"It has at least the same chance," Andrea muttered mutinously.

"You cannot have given this proper thought. Midnight *and* a church. Both are bound to be powerful influences."

"But what about that silly incantation? Really, Emmy"—Andrea started to laugh—"it's all too ridiculous. The very thought of the two of us running around the church twelve times chanting 'I sow hempseed, hempseed I sow. He that loves me best come after me now' sends me into whoops. Why, if anyone hears us, they'll come after us, all right. With straitjackets."

"Very well then. If that's your attitude, I'll go alone." Emmy sipped her tea in silence while managing to create an atmosphere of betrayal and martyrdom.

Andrea sighed and capitulated. "You know very well that I'll not allow you to do that. Midnight it is."

Actually, it was a quarter before that hour when two shadowy figures stole into the churchyard. Andrea did not know whether to be glad or sorry for the moonlight. It had certainly made it easier to find their way down the carriage drive and along the road that led to the village, but it illuminated the stone church with its square tower a bit too well for her liking, not to mention that it made the marble gravestones in the adjoining cemetery seemed positively alive. Still, she reflected practically, they'd have good visibility for their lunatic run and shouldn't turn their ankles on unseen stones or go careening into bushes. And no one with equally good visibility was apt to be abroad, she hoped, at this hour of the night.

"All right then, let's go."

Emmy also seemed to be affected by the atmosphere. For there was nothing in the spell that involved holding hands. Indeed, this made it much more difficult to run, though Andrea had to admit that the contact was comforting.

"I sow hempseed, hempseed I sow," the two girls muttered under their breath, partly to conserve that commodity and perhaps so as not to disturb the sleeping occupants of the graveyard. It was Emmy who set the pace, and whereas Andrea was sympathetic to her desire to get the whole daft business over with, she did wonder as they flew by the entrance for the third time—"I sow hempseed, hempseed I sow"—if perhaps they should try to save themselves a bit.

Her forebodings were borne out, for on the seventh circuit, Emmy suddenly clutched her side with a shriek and doubled over.

"What is it?" The creepy atmosphere kept Andrea's alarmed voice at whisper level.

"I've got a stitch in my side. I can't go on." To reinforce that statement, she sank down upon the lowest church step. "You'll have to finish without me."

"I'll do no such thing. I'm taking you home."

"You can't stop now." Emmy actually managed to wail at low volume. "At least one of us has to finish or we'll never know whether the spell works or not."

"I already know. Do you think you can walk

slowly, Emmy? Frankly, this place gives me the shivers."

"Andrea, please." Tears were in Emmy's voice. "You've only five more circuits left. And the longer you delay, the greater the chance of the spell being broken. I'm sure you have to do it all at once, not in installments."

"Oh, very well."

She could finish the silly business faster by agreeing rather than arguing. Andrea resumed the run, quickening her pace. "I sow hempseed, hempseed I sow." She had rounded the back of the church and was halfway along the graveyard wall. "I sow hemp—" Her shriek was cut off by a gloved hand clapped over her mouth as she was jerked behind the shrubbery and backed against the chill stone.

"For God's sake, don't screech again and I'll unstop your mouth," a male voice whispered. He could have saved himself the further trouble of identifying himself. "It's me, Blakeney." From the moment he'd breathed into her ear, she had not had the slightest doubt of his identity.

"Just what do you think you're doing?" she hissed indignantly when, as promised, he'd freed her mouth.

"That was to have been my question," he whispered back. "For of all the idiotic performances this has to take the prize." He suddenly began to shake with silent laughter. "I sow hempseed', for God's sake."

"I'm glad you find me so amusing," she replied as haughtily as she could, given the fact that she was still pressed tightly against him. "Now, if you'll release me, I'll—"

"You'll what? Continue running like a dog in fits?

94

Really, Andrea, I always knew that my cousin was one small step removed from a bedlamite, but I did give you more credit."

"I'll grant that all this does look queer—well, then, *is* queer—but Emmy doesn't want to leave till one of us completes this nonsense. And she has a stitch in her side and I don't like to leave her sitting in the cold. So if you will kindly turn me loose . . ."

"Listen, in a minute or so this place is going to be swarming with men and you don't want to be found here. I doubt they'll wish to be recognized."

"What on earth—"

"Come on. I'll explain later. The thing you need to do right now is to get Emmy and cross the road into the trees." They were moving stealthily along the church wall. "Once everyone's inside, you girls run home. But keep in the shadows. And be careful. They might post a lookout, though I doubt it."

"Who are they?" Andrea was totally alarmed.

"Just a bunch of my farmers with delusions of grandeur. Zach Cannon's trying to make revolutionaries out of them, God help him."

They had reached the front of the church, where they froze at the sound of a distant whistle. He peered cautiously around the corner and chuckled softly. "Emmy's streaking across the road like the devil's behind her. Good girl! She's hiding in the trees. Let's hope she stays there. Now you go. Run!"

Andrea hesitated. "But aren't you coming?" She could not quite keep the alarm out of her voice.

"No. I came here to find out what's going on, not"—he choked—"to sow hempseed. Let me look again and make certain the coast is clear." He cautiously stepped out far enough to see the road in both directions but was back beside her in a trice. "Too late. I see lanterns. Come on."

He grabbed her hand and pulled her swiftly along the wall in back of the shrubbery toward the rear of the church. "Don't move. Don't talk. Don't breathe," he cautioned as he released her to turn to the church window just behind him and try to force it open. "Damnation," he muttered as it refused to budge.

Andrea could now see occasional flashes of light through the thick foliage and hear the low sound of hurrying footsteps. She eased along the wall to Blakeney's side just as the second window, left unbolted, yielded to pressure. He adjusted it to the merest crack, then turned to push her down into a sitting position beneath the window. "I told you not to move," he breathed.

"I wanted to hear, too."

"Well, it will be warmer this way." He put an arm around her and pulled her close. She was on the point of wresting herself free when a warning pressure on her shoulder caused her to freeze and hold her breath. People were already within the church.

All she could hear, strain though she might, was a babble of men's low voices. The words were unintelligible. She gathered they were merely greeting one another. And the general tone seemed subdued, whether from fear or from a consciousness of their clandestine invasion of sacred premises she had no way of knowing.

Just as she was wondering if it would be safe to sneak out of the bushes and run across the road to Emmy, who must be quaking in terror there all alone, a clear authoritative voice rose above the others. "The meeting will come to order."

Beside her, Blakeney was rising slowly, a hand placed firmly on her head to warn her not to follow suit.

She had no need to peer through the window, as was his intent, to recognize the voice that was holding forth. Zach Cannon's, once heard, was not easily forgotten.

He proved to be an impassioned orator. His words were like sparks, meant to ignite the tinder of his listeners' discontent. He spoke of the grievances of the English working class throughout the land. He spoke of the heinous corn laws. Of the bread riots that had broken out in dozens of towns across the country where work had suddenly become scarce. He spoke of homeless veterans, men who had fought on land and on sea, now forced to drift through the towns and along the highways, reduced to the most humiliating types of odd jobs because there was no honest work for them to do.

His mesmerizing voice took on new overtones of bitterness as he contrasted their lot to that of the idle rich. The idle rich—epitomized by the Prince Regent. He dwelled on the Regent's extravagances, emphasizing the opulent pleasure palace being built in Brighton. He painted a sordid picture of the prince's dissipated private life. He went on to castigate the Parliament for enriching themselves while heartlessly taxing the poor. And he offered his listeners a solution to all their ills. "I'm here to recruit you, men," he thundered, "into the vanguard of those who will rise and save our country for those very people who have made it great. Who among you wants Bread to feed the hungry, Truth

97

to overcome the oppressors, and Justice to punish crimes?"

Both sacred atmosphere and caution were now flung to the winds. There was a stamping of feet, and the shouted huzzahs rattled the windows.

"Who wants every man in England to have a vote?" The shouts and stamping intensified.

"Who wants to see the land divided equally amongst those who till it?"

The crescendo swelled.

"And if they won't give us what we want, shall we not take it?"

At that point there was pandemonium.

After some moments Cannon quieted down the crowd. "I am here, men, to administer the oath that will make you members of the Spencean Society. Let those too craven to join our brotherhood leave now—first swearing never to disclose a word to anyone, neither wife nor sweetheart, about what has taken place here this night. Betrayal will bring retribution, swift and terrible."

There was a long and pregnant pause. Andrea strained her ears but heard no sound of retreating footsteps.

"Stout fellows!" The leader spoke with satisfaction. "Now we will take the oath on the Bible and in this holy place pledge our fidelity to the brotherhood. We shall begin with the back rows there and work our way to the front. You first, Ned Barker."

Lord Blakeney watched at the window a bit longer, then sank back down on the ground next to Andrea. "Regular little Orator Hunt, ain't he?" he whispered. She could hear the laughter in his voice and concluded that he was totally insane.

"They'll likely be a while, for they've brought along some cider jugs, lacking ceremonial wine, I gather. Might as well make ourselves comfortable while we outwait them." So saying, he enfolded her in his arms again, wrapping his greatcoat snugly around her.

She did, of course, long to offer aggressive resistance. Especially when he tilted her chin up and began to kiss her, tenderly and expertly. First the ear, which she naïvely considered to be a mistaken target until his warm breath and teasing lips began to have a strange effect upon her traitorous body and make her wonder if it would not be, everything considered, far less dangerous to struggle free and be discovered eavesdropping by the Spenceans than to meekly accept the assault upon her senses that was going on.

But the exploring mouth had begun to trace a searing path by way of her eyelids, down her cheek, and inexorably to her lips. Upon its arrival there she was lost to further speculation.

Time had no meaning. The voices and the sound of footsteps inside the church faded away. The icy night air, the cold stone behind her were of no consequence. She was enveloped in a warm, soft glow.

Even when Blakeney, with obvious reluctance, ceased his ungentlemanly behavior, he continued to hold her close. Her head rested on his shoulder and she snuggled against him and drifted off to sleep.

She had no sense of the passage of time. "Andrea. Andrea, wake up." She was being gently shaken. "It's safe to go now. The newly formed chapter of the Spencean Society has adjourned and staggered off toward home."

It took a moment for her to realize just where she was. She gazed blankly upward into a face with a rather sheepish smile, clearly revealed in the stark moonlight.

Memory flooded back and with it a humiliating rush of blood to her face. "You really are a rake, aren't you?" she said bitterly. "You can't be around any woman, can you, without making love."

"Any woman?" He rose stiffly from their cramped, cold retreat and pulled her to her feet. "Must you be quite so hard on me, my dear Miss Prior? I would not make love to just any woman. Give me credit for a bit of taste."

"What I gave you credit for is being a complete and utter libertine who took advantage of the situation."

"Well, yes, I collect that's true, at least in part," he said reflectively. "But pray bear this in mind, dear, proper Miss Prior. We might simply have sat there, bored, virtuous, and freezing, in the bushes. But thanks to my resourcefulness, you must admit that the time passed quite pleasantly. And tomorrow, when you realize that you are entirely free from the grippe and rheumatism, I do believe you will actually come to thank me."

Andrea was not quite rendered speechless by this preposterous pronouncement, for she did manage a toplofty "Go to the devil, Lord Blakeney!" as she pushed her way through the bushes and headed toward home.

Chapter Twelve

"*I don't suppose you could consider all this a great* adventure that you'll recall with pleasure in years to come?"

He had hurried to catch up with her and had adapted his long stride to her near-to-running pace.

"I could not."

"I was afraid of that. Well, allow me to point out that there's no need for such unseemly haste. I can't see that it really matters whether you're caught sneaking back in at two o'clock or at half-past."

"Allow me to point out that if my pace bothers you it is not necessary for you to keep up with it."

"Ah, but it is. Can't let you go home alone, you know. After all, I am a gentleman."

Her hoot was eloquent, if unrefined.

"I must say," he mused as they passed through the Kingswood gates, "you are exceptionally athletic for a female. All that racing around the church. What was your count, by the by?"

She did not deign to answer.

"Well, I realize that due to circumstances you didn't make your goal. But surely you came close?"

More silence.

"Never mind. For it was your speed that impressed me far more than your endurance. Tell me. Did the proximity of the graveyard have any bearing on your performance?"

Once again he paused for an answer that was not forthcoming.

"And after all that sprinting, here you are, at it again, out to set a walking record, I do believe. But then, perhaps," he mused, "I'm giving you too much credit. After all, you did have a nice nap in between these extremes of exercise."

She stopped in her tracks and whirled on him. "Lord Blakeney, I do not wish to be reminded of my wanton conduct. And if you had the slightest sensibility, you would realize it. What's more, if you ever, *ever*, tell anyone of what transpired tonight, I'll—I'll . . ." She ran down like an unwound clock.

"You'll what?" He sounded genuinely interested.

Her only answer was to set off again, almost at a run.

"Steady on there." He reached out to take her by the upper arm and slow her down to a more sedate pace. "No call to upset yourself. The question was academic. Of course I'll not tell anyone." There was injury in his tone. "You know, you are a bit hard on me, Miss Prior. While I don't claim to be a saint, I'm not the villain you take me for. Don't you think you might be carrying your childhood prejudices a bit far? After all, we're both grown-up now."

102

"Yes," she retorted between clenched teeth, "but only one of us is mature."

"Oh, well, then. But don't despair. You've barely left the schoolroom. You'll catch up in time."

Her glare was eloquent in the moonlight. They had reached the path to the dower house. "Good night, Lord Blakeney. Under the circumstances, I don't think it advisable for you to see me to the door."

"Hmmm. You do have a point. Anyone seeing us out together and alone at this scandalous hour might decide the only proper thing for us to do is marry."

"When pigs fly!"

"Then you know about our breeding efforts here. I am amazed. I had no idea you'd interest yourself in a thing like that. But even though we're creating a bit of a stir in pig circles with the new breed we're developing, it's probably a bit much to expect wings. No, you mustn't pin your hopes on flight."

"Very amusing." Her tone was venomous. "Good night, Lord Blakeney."

He stopped her leaving by grasping her shoulders and turning her toward him. "It's my turn to beg silence, Andrea." He spoke quite seriously. "I don't want my grandmother to know what our laborers are up to. Tell my cousin not to speak of it, will you?"

"Emmy's hardly likely to admit that we sneaked out of the house."

"Oh, but you never know. She's chuckleheaded enough for anything."

"You're quite mistaken, of course. But I will convey your message. Now, if you'll release me." She looked politely at each of his hands in turn.

"Oh, what the devil!" His solemn face broke into an impish grin. "Might as well be hanged for a sheep as a lamb."

He pulled her tight against him, and though she quickly turned her head to avoid his lips, they found their target with practiced ease.

This time she thought she knew what to expect. She was not the least bit fooled by the meteor shower that fell around her. Her own senses, and not the heavens, were producing this phenomenon. Even so, she was aware of clinging to one of the capes of his greatcoat for the support she did not trust her knees to give. And a tender glow was once more enveloping her, a sensation at complete variance with the nature of its source. It wasn't fair, some almost-drowned inner voice protested weakly. She had dreamed of this. Being clasped in strong male arms and kissed to the very edge of distraction and beyond, in just the way the novels she and Emmy had read beneath the bed covers at school had described it. But it was Sir Galahad that she had dreamed of. And here was Mordred turning her into an abandoned woman totally unlike herself. Could this lack of self-control be an inheritance from her father? The thought was horrifying. Andrea mustered one last burst of will and gave Blakeney a shove that parted them completely. The feeling of rectitude she experienced from this superhuman endeavor was short-lived as it slowly dawned on her that, once again, his lips had released hers first.

"Good night, Andrea," he said huskily. "And quit berating yourself. Is it so bad to discover that you're only human?"

"Yes."

She turned and ran for the back entrance to the dower house as though all the graveyard demons were swooping after her.

It was too much to hope that Emmy would be in bed asleep. In fact, she was pacing back and forth in their chamber in a state of near hysteria.

"Oh, Andrea, I was sure those brutes had killed you!" she gasped as soon as the door closed softly behind her friend. She rushed to squeeze the breath out of Andrea in a frantic hug.

"Oh, come now." Andrea extracted herself and went to hover over the dying fire. "You're letting your imagination run away with you. Those 'brutes' as you call them are the same men who have been working your farms forever. They would never harm us."

"Oh, no? Then why were you and Blake hiding from them? I saw him there. He came out from behind the church just as that mob was coming and then slipped back again. Hiding was what you two were doing all this time, was it not?" She gave her friend a rather peculiar look.

Andrea did her best to appear nonchalant. "He had come to try to find out what was going on. And, naturally, he could not have done so if we'd been discovered."

"There, you see!" Hysteria threatened to increase Emmy's volume, and Andrea put a warning finger to her lips. "Blake realizes that we'll all be murdered in our beds. You wait and see."

"Nonsense. From what I could overhear, all they are planning is to refuse to plant the spring crops this year. Which could certainly be calamitous but has nothing to do with murdering the aristocracy."

"It's the first step. You mark my words." Emmy resumed her pacing. "Remember the Luddites? I doubt they were taken seriously at first, either. And everyone says they left huge caches of arms hidden underground, just waiting for some English Jacobins to rise and claim them."

"Oh, for goodness' sake, Emmy. Get ahold of yourself. The Luddites were nowhere near here."

"It doesn't matter. Radicalism is spreading. I tell you, it will be the French Revolution all over again."

"Fustian. You've let your nerves run away with you. What you need is sleep. Things will look much better in the morning. Come now." Andrea was scrambling into her nightdress. "Let's go to bed. The fire is almost done for."

As they crawled, shivering, under the covers, Emmy said, "I'll speak to Grandmama. She'll know how to nip this business in the bud. She says that Blake is far too lenient and progressive with his workers. He needs a firmer hand."

"Oh, no, you mustn't!" Andrea sat up in alarm. "Lord Blakeney asked me specifically to tell you to say nothing to your grandmother."

"As if I care a fig about his instructions."

"Perhaps not, as a general rule. But do you propose to explain to your grandmother just how we came by this information?"

"Oh."

There was a long silence while Emmy appeared to think that over. "Oh, do lie down, Andrea. You're letting in the cold." And as Andrea complied, she gave in between yawns. "Oh, very well then, I won't speak to Grandmama. But what I will do is have a

106

talk with Blake the very first thing tomorrow morning and make sure that he seeks her advice."

Andrea gave token approval to Emmy's plan though she privately thought that the chances of Lord Blakeney's paying any attention to anyone's advice, let alone a female's—even a female as formidable as the Dowager Lady Blakeney—were slim, indeed.

"But would you promise me one more thing?" she asked as Emmy turned on her stomach and prepared to sleep.

"What's that?" The question was muffled.

"Promise me that tonight will be the absolute last of your Valentine's charms. Not only is the whole notion absurd in the extreme, but tonight's little excursion bordered on the lunatic."

"Ummmm . . ."

She sighed to herself as her friend's rhythmical breathing indicated that she was fast asleep. Andrea turned on her side and tried to follow Emmy's example. But her mind continued to dwell on the various lunacies of the past few days. And she could not believe that she had allowed her friend to involve her in such nonsense. Hard-boiled eggs and bay leaves. Hearts drawn from urns. And then pinned to sleeves. There was no denying that her dear Emmy could be as goosish as they came.

Andrea pulled the covers up over her ears. The disturbing thing, of course, was the way Lord Blakeney had kept intruding himself into this silly business. Still, though, she reasoned, he had not actually drawn her heart out of the urn. The fact that he had been the only male who had not participated, and hers had been the only heart undrawn, did not mean that her valentine had been intended for him. In fact, his nonparticipation had nullified the whole daft procedure. And as for this insane escapade tonight, it was mere coincidence that he was the first man she saw after she had run around the church. . . .

But no, wait! She had not completed the spell. She was supposed to have run around the church twelve times and she had gotten nowhere near that number when he had grabbed her. So of course it didn't count!

The relief that reflection gave her was overwhelming. At least it was until she reflected that by taking any of this ridiculous business seriously, she, quite possibly, was growing every bit as bird-witted as her dearest friend.

On that lowering thought Andrea, at last, drifted off to sleep.

Chapter Thirteen

If Andrea had hoped that Emmy would forget her fears in the cold light of day, she was disappointed. Nor was she able to dissuade her friend from conferring with her cousin even though she pointed out the impropriety of calling, unchaperoned, at what was momentarily a bachelor residence.

"Nonsense. Kingswood Hall is really my home. I'll go there whenever I choose." Emmy's face was set stubbornly.

Yes, but you needn't drag me along. Andrea kept the retort to herself. For she was honest enough to admit that it was not the impropriety that bothered her. It was the awkwardness—to use the champion of all understatements—of seeing Lord Blakeney again.

Still, it had to be done. And the sooner the better, perhaps. Like getting right back up on a horse once you have fallen off. She flinched at the analogy.

Abandoning one's principles to behave like a loose woman was hardly to be compared to an accidental tumble off a horse.

But the fact remained. She could not avoid his lordship forever. And one thing was certain. He'd not be dwelling on the incident the way that she was. Why, in a day or so he would be hard-pressed to remember just which of his gaggle of goosish females he had made love to while the radicals plotted. Somehow that thought was more humiliating than comforting.

But he had to be faced. For no matter how she might long to flee to France, to London, to anywhere, she knew that she could not. Lady Blakeney's offer to help her start a school seemed her only opportunity in a future that looked grim indeed. And while it was certainly unfortunate that the school had to be located on Lord Blakeney's estate, it was by no means fatal. For she really had nothing to fear from that particular quarter. She was hardly likely ever to be alone again in a churchyard at midnight with Lord Casanova. This reflection made good sense. But all the reasoning in the world could not hide the fact that she herself, and not Lord Blakeney, just might be the enemy.

Any hope she had entertained, as they'd hurried up the drive toward the manor house, that his lordship would be off and gone was dashed as soon as the butler ushered them into the Hall. Lord Blakeney, wearing a dressing gown of dark red printed silk (that surely his mother must have given him) was coming down the stairs. He paused in midflight to stare at them sardonically. "Ah, the gorgons. And to what do I owe the honor?"

"Blakeney, we must talk to you."

Emmy's unaccustomed gravity caused her cousin to shift his eyes from Andrea, who was studiously examining the suit of armor in the corner of the stairway, and give her his full attention. "Well, that sounds ominous," he observed.

Oh, my heavens, Andrea thought, panicked, I'll bet a monkey he thinks Emmy's going to rake him over the coals about his behavior toward me last night.

"Well, ladies"—he was ambling down the stairs—"shall we retire to the drawing room for this conference? Higgens, fetch us tea, there's a good fellow."

"Oh, no, not for me, thank you." Andrea still couldn't force herself to look directly at him. She only prayed that if her cheeks were red, he'd blame it on the frigid weather. "I'll not intrude in a family discussion. If I may, I'd like to see your library. And perhaps borrow a book or two?"

"As many as you like." He sounded amused, confound him. But his face was perfectly straight when she did give him a censorious look. "You may, of course, have to blow the dust off. God knows, the books get little use these days. The library's . . . But, then, you know where it is. How could I forget all those summers when you graced us with your presence?" He did grin then, making her long to throttle him.

Her relief at having escaped with her dignity more or less intact proved to be short-lived. She had closed the library door and was leaning back against it to give needed support to her quaking knees. She was in the act of closing her eyes for a moment of quiet recovery when they were jarred wide open.

Lord Gresham, seated at the library table, enveloped by a cloud of cigar smoke, lowered the newspaper he was reading to stare at her. "Oh, I say"— he pushed back his chair and scrambled to his feet— "this is a pleasant surprise."

She could have screamed from pure vexation. Next to Lord Blakeney, and indeed running that obnoxious gentleman a very close second, the person she was most desirous of avoiding was Lord Gresham.

"Oh, pray don't let me disturb you. Do go on with your reading, sir. I've only come for a book, then I'll be out of your way. I do know how gentlemen hate to be interrupted from their newspapers."

Dark mahogany shelves lined the room from floor to ceiling. She walked swiftly to the nearest one and snatched down a book as she was speaking. The fact that she had chosen *Tom Jones*, which Miss Monkhouse had declared unfit for ladies, quite failed to register.

"Nonsense."

He stood behind her, almost pressing her against the shelves and reeking of cigar smoke and other odors she did not care to identity. His lordship was obviously none too fastidious in his personal hygiene.

"Come talk to me, Miss Prior." He took her arm and propelled her toward the sofa that faced a crackling fireplace. "Can't tell you how good it is to see a sympathetic face. Never so bored in my entire life. Completely beyond me how people can bury themselves in these godforsaken places and be content to rusticate their lives away."

"Well, the country is not to everyone's taste," Andrea said diplomatically as she tried to inch away from him. Since he had placed her by the sofa arm and then sat close beside her, there was little room for this maneuver. "What I don't understand is why you stay on, Lord Gresham, if you find Kingswood so tedious."

"Oh, do you not, young lady?" He leered at her suggestively. "Well, I don't mind saying that I'd leave this very minute if you would agree to come with me."

"I?" She turned toward him in astonishment, then found their faces much too close and quickly looked away. "I certainly have no reason to go to London. You have forgotten that my father is abroad."

"Of course I've not forgotten. In fact, that's me very point. I plan on giving you a reason to go to the metropolis. For now that your father has blotted his copybook, so to speak—or to speak plainer, has gambled your fortune away—there's no use your hoping for a decent sort of marriage. Oh, with your looks I don't doubt some cit might make you an offer, but no member of the ton is going to be rash enough to propose marriage to a pauper. No, my dear Miss Prior, your best hope for the kind of life you might have had, with a gentleman to look after you, is in a more unconventional arrangement. I'm a very wealthy man, m'dear. Don't mind saying I was plump in the pocket even before I married, and being leg-shackled's more than doubled me income. So you'll never want for any luxury with me, m'dear. Can't set you up in a fashionable part of town, of course," he added regretfully. "Wouldn't be at all the thing. But I promise you that the house will be every bit as elegantly furnished as any in Grovesnor Square. And as for gowns and jewels, why, no lady in London will be able to hold you a candle."

At first Andrea had listened with astonishment.

This reaction was rapidly turning to rage. "Do I understand you correctly, Lord Gresham?" Her tone might have caused icicles to form. "You are offering me carte blanche?"

"If that's the way you choose to phrase it."

"Is there some other way?"

"No, damme, there isn't. Can't expect me to go down on one knee, now, can you? Even if I wasn't already leg-shackled, and with an heir by this time I should think, it still wouldn't be the thing, as I've just explained. Your father, don't you see. Puts you beyond the pale for marriage. But"—he brightened—"if you wish me to say I've lost me heart to you, by God, I can do that. Can't recall ever being so taken with a female. Oh, I grant you, I've been bored past all endurance from rusticating in this hole, but believe me, Miss Prior—Andrea—that ain't it at all. You mustn't think that you're just a whim on me part and that when I get back to the city I'll change me mind. No, by George, I can't wait to show you off in Rotten Row. Did I mention I have a spanking new high-perch phaeton? By God, the heads will turn when we tool through the park in that!"

"Indeed? And what will your wife be doing in the meantime?"

"How should I know?" The question seemed to mystify him. "Should think that she'll be taken up with her brat. Females generally are, I understand. But what Lady Gresham does has nothing to say in the matter. If you're thinking she may kick up a dust, you can forget it. She'll not even acknowledge your existence. Take me word for it. Wouldn't be good ton, you know."

"How comforting."

Her sarcasm was lost on Lord Gresham. "Yes, I

thought it would be. No, m'dear, you don't have to worry your pretty head about me going back on me word to you."

"Believe me, Lord Gresham, I do not."

"Good. It's settled then. When can you be ready? Far as I'm concerned I can't shake the dust of this curst place off me boots a moment too soon."

"Well, we're certainly in agreement there, sir. You can't leave too soon for me, either. But as for your loathsome proposition"—the anger she'd been controlling turned from ice to steam—"all that I can say is that when my father returns to England, you'll be very fortunate indeed, sir, if he does not call you out!"

Lord Gresham looked more perplexed than disturbed by her reaction. "You really are all abroad, Andrea m'dear. Didn't realize that you ain't got the slightest notion just how deep into the River Tick your papa is. Lord bless me, he's going to be relieved to learn that I've taken you under me wing. And if he's what's bothering you, I'll not mind slipping him a bit of blunt now and then. Though you mustn't think I'll support his gaming habits. Couldn't do that. He'd ruin us in a fortnight. No use to wrap the matter up in clean linen, for that's how gamblers are. Now what do you say, Andrea?"

"Lord Gresham, you have left me speechless. There is not one thing I *can* say that is suitable to cross a lady's lips. So let me content myself by wishing you good day."

She tried to rise, but he leaned over and pinned her back against the armrest with his massive body.

"So that's the way it is, is it? Should've known not to waste me breath trying to reason with a female. There's just one thing they understand."

Andrea tried to escape him but was helpless against the weight that was pressing the breath out of her body. She did manage one cry for help just before the repellent, slack mouth pressed down upon hers, and she succeeded in raking her nails across the side of his face after the fact. Lord Gresham's only reaction to this attack was to grab the offending hand in a viselike grip and increase his ardor.

Andrea had once been proud of the fact that she had never swooned in her life. This now became a reason for despair. Her only hope for oblivion was if the corpulent Gresham should smother the life right out of her, a consummation that was devoutly to be wished. But before that could happen, she rallied all her strength to push against the behemoth mass for one last time.

To her utter amazement, it worked. Lord Gresham was propelled off her like a boulder out of a catapult. She sat up, gasping for breath, and saw Lord Blakeney, with one hand grasping the back of Gresham's collar and with fire in his eyes, draw back a fist and then slam it into his astonished victim's face. The thud was sickening. Blood spurted from Gresham's nose. A female screamed. Andrea chastised herself for being so hen-hearted, then discovered that the frightened shriek had come from Emmy. She heard a rush of running footsteps and then the library door burst open. A lovely middle-aged, modishly dressed lady paused on the threshold drinking in the scene. Mr. Austen and Sir Nigel Lyncomb stood, open-mouthed, behind her.

Chapter
Fourteen

"*I can see that I have not arrived home a moment too soon.*"

"Your timing is awkward, as always, Mama."

Lord Blakeney massaged his fist as he turned to face his parent. Beau Austen had rushed to Gresham's side and was attempting to stanch the flow of blood with his handkerchief. Sir Nigel was seeing to Emmy even though that young lady seemed to have recovered from her initial shock and was now looking more entertained than overcome. Miss Prior was left to adjust her clothes and smooth her hair and deal with her acute embarrassment the best she could.

The final phase of Andrea's agenda was not aided by the fact that Lady Blakeney was surveying her with marked disapproval. "The young person who precipitated this unseemly brawling is, I collect, Charlie Prior's daughter?"

"No need to take against Andrea, Aunt," Emmy protested, jumping up from the chair where Sir Nigel had solicitously placed her. "She has practically nothing to do with all this. What I mean to say is, Blake has been longing to draw Gresham's cork ever since he broke Horatio's leg. Any old excuse would have done him."

"Why, thank you, cousin," Lord Blakeney said dryly.

Andrea could have echoed this reaction even while she acknowledged the truth of Emmy's statement.

"Well, that can, perhaps, explain my son's conduct, but it hardly explains Miss Prior's unladylike behavior. Hasn't your father done enough damage to the family name, Miss Prior, without your help?"

"Aunt!"

Emmy's gasp was drowned by her cousin's preemptive "That will do, Mama. And to think that I used to be known as the boorish member of the family."

"Still are, if you want me opinion." From his seat on the floor Lord Gresham chimed in thickly through Beau Austen's handkerchief. "Seems to me somebody in this lunatic asylum ought to send for a doctor."

"Oh, for God's sake, you're all right." Blakeney threw him a disgusted look. "Don't think I even broke your nose, more's the pity. You don't need a quack. But I will ring for a servant to clean you up *and*," he added pointedly, "pack for you."

"I must apologize for my son's complete lack of civility, Lord Gresham. And for his present dishabille." Her gaze roamed from Blakeney's dressing gown to Andrea's embarrassed face and seemed to connect the two. "He has always been a source of despair to me. But he is right in one thing. You will wish to leave right away."

"Damned right. Can't wait to see the last of this cursed place."

"Well, yes, I see. But that was not my meaning. I had wished to tell you that your wife has given birth."

"Has she, b'gad?" Gresham removed the bloody handkerchief from his nose while everyone else looked appalled at that organ's swelling. "And what was it?"

"A healthy little daughter."

"A female! Well, if that ain't the damned final straw. Couldn't get me an heir, oh, no! Should have known she'd bungle the thing."

No one seemed to know quite what to say to this bitter declaration. It might have been tact on Lord Blakeney's part, though more likely not, that caused him to change the subject.

"To what do we owe the honor of your presence, Mama?" he asked abruptly.

"Let's just say that some maternal instinct warned me that I was needed at home." Lady Blakeney looked pointedly at Miss Prior once again.

"Fustian. Why, *really*, are you here? And more to the point, how long do you plan to stay?"

"I'm touched by your filial concern, Hadrian."

"Don't call me that," Blakeney growled, while his cousin snickered, "Hadrian," beneath her breath.

"Whyever not? It's a splendid name. Though, I'll grant you, a bit patrician. But, then, when you were born I had high hopes."

"I repeat, how long a visit are you planning?"

"This is not a visit. I am home to stay."

"But you can't be!" Emmy was glaring at her aunt indignantly. "The Season's just beginning. Why, I could have made my come-out if we had known you would not be using the house."

"As you may recall, niece, I offered to sponsor your come-out."

"Oh, my God, don't start that up again," Blakeney groaned as two servants entered with a basin and some cloths, making it obvious that they were well aware of the preceding events.

Andrea rose from the sofa and murmured, "Emeline, we should be going." She carefully avoided looking at Lord Gresham as she stepped around him.

"I'll walk you ladies home," Sir Nigel volunteered.

Beau Austen had gladly turned over his feeble ministrations to the servants. They began to sponge off Gresham's face. "I'll also offer myself as escort," he said.

"There ain't time for you two to play Romeo," Gresham snapped. "We're leaving as soon as me things can be packed and the carriage fetched."

"Er, g-go on without me, old f-fellow," Sir Nigel stammered.

Beau Austen hesitated a long moment before declaring that he would be staying on as well.

"I don't think that's a wise idea, Beau." Gresham glared.

"Well, old fellow, you know how matters stand. It's none too comfortable for me in London at the moment."

"It will be a damned sight less comfortable if you don't come with me. For if you choose to remain under the same roof with *him*"—he jerked a thumb

Lord Blakeney's way—"why, then, by God, we're finished. I wash me hands of you."

Beau Austen's hesitation was even longer this time. He looked Emmy's way, but she was engrossed in putting on the cloak a servant had fetched and would not meet his eyes. He gave a heavy sigh. "I'm sorry you feel like that, old fellow. But Blake and I do go back a long way, you understand."

"Well, then, you can both go to the devil!" Leaning heavily on a footman's arm and mustering all the dignity that a swelling proboscis allowed him, Lord Gresham left the room.

Lord Blakeney, ignoring his mother's aura of disapproval and trading his dressing gown for a greatcoat, also decided to join the procession to the dower house, falling in beside Andrea as the other two gentlemen attached themselves to his cousin. Emmy was doing her best to appear fragile and distraught, in need of a great deal of solicitude.

"Would you look at her?" Blake watched the trio ahead in disgust as Andrea, unlike his cousin, managed to descend the hall's steep marble steps without assistance. "She should take her shrinking-violet act to Drury Lane."

Though she would have thought herself incapable of such an action, Andrea laughed. "You must admit," she observed as they watched both gentlemen tenderly guide Emmy around a small tree branch downed on the carriage path, "that it is working."

"Yes, the poor sapskulls."

"They are not sapskulls. Your cousin is everything a gentleman could wish for. As you'd realize if you had not grown up with her."

"Perhaps. If your taste runs to rattlepates."

"Emmy's no such thing." Andrea sprang to her

friend's defense, glad of the biting air and the present debate that took her mind away from recent humiliations. "Besides, since you brought it up, it has been my observation that gentlemen do not value intellect in ladies. Would you not agree?"

"Never having known any with that commodity," he said, grinning down at her, "I really couldn't say."

"You're trying to make me rise to the bait instead of answering me honestly," she retorted. "You're well acquainted with your grandmother."

"Touché. But even you aren't about to say that Emmy takes after Grandmama."

"Who knows? It's early days yet. The Dowager Lady Blakeney could have been very much the same at Emmy's age."

"My God, what a thought. I'd best run up ahead and warn my friends."

Andrea laughed again at his mock horror, but his eyes had narrowed as he watched the threesome. "Beau's hopeless as a gambler," he remarked, perhaps to himself. "He has backed the wrong horse as usual."

"I don't think I quite understand." Andrea, too, directed her attention on the group ahead. Emmy was gazing up at Beau with rapt attention as he spoke to her. Sir Nigel was now walking a bit apart, apparently uninterested in his friend's conversation. "It's obvious, is it not, that Emmy is quite smitten. Surely you approve?"

He shrugged. "I simply think he'd have been wiser not to alienate Gresham."

"That toad! How can you, of all people, say so?"

"Oh, I heartily agree that Gresham's a wrong 'un. But I'm not sure that Beau can afford to antagonize him. But that's his affair. I'm just thankful to have seen the last of his whey-faced lordship."

Andrea was forced back once more into the painful episode she'd tried momentarily to blot from her mind. "I have not yet thanked you," she said awkwardly, "for . . . doing what you did back there. Of course I am sure Emmy was right. Assaulting Lord Gresham was a thing you longed to do."

"And you just furnished the excuse? Oh, well, so much for chivalry. I grant you that knight-errantry is not exactly my style."

"I wasn't trying to diminish what you did, Lord Blakeney." She turned her head away when, to her horror, she felt tears stinging her eyes. "Believe me, whatever your motives, I am very, very grateful."

He stopped in his tracks and pulled her to a halt beside him. Placing a gloved hand on her chin, he turned her head to face him. With a herculean effort she mastered the tears. "Did that bastard hurt you?" he asked roughly.

"N-no. It was just . . . disgusting."

"Yes." He gazed down at her thoughtfully. "I can see how it would be. I suppose it is difficult—at times—to be a beautiful woman."

"Surely you mean gargoyle?"

"Touché again." He clutched his breast and staggered as though run through by a rapier. "But getting back to Gresham—"

"Must we? I'm doing my utmost to forget."

"What exactly did he have in mind? Well, that was fairly obvious, of course, though I can't believe that even Gresham would go so far as to rape you."

"Lord Blakeney!"

"Oh, come now. No call to turn missish on me."

"No, sensibility is a luxury I can no longer afford,

it seems." Her voice was bitter. "Since you ask, he offered me carte blanche."

"Did he, by God! That—" Lord Blakeney's string of epithets seemed to turn the frosty air bright blue. In spite of her embarrassment Andrea was a bit impressed. "I should have killed him while I had the chance," he finished.

"Thank you," she said dryly. "But the incident was hardly worth a trip to the Tyburn tree, or wherever they now hang murderers. It's the sort of thing that unprotected females must learn to expect."

"You weren't unprotected. You were under my roof."

"How chivalrous." Her tone spoke volumes.

"Devil take your sarcasm," he said angrily. "If you're trying to lump Gresham and me together, well, I'll have you know that what happened between you and me in the churchyard and his damned offer of carte blanche are not the same sort of thing at all."

She was glad that the others were now waiting for them at the gateway to the dower house and she was not forced to answer. For all that she could have done with honesty was to admit the truth of what he'd just said. Being made love to by Lord Blakeney and by Lord Gresham were not the same sorts of experience at all. From daylight to dark was not contrast enough to adequately describe the difference.

Chapter
Fifteen

"**M**y *dearest daughter . . .*"
Andrea read the letter for the dozenth time, then laid it in her lap. She gazed, unseeing, out the window of the bedchamber, where she had retreated to read it in private. How strange life was. A simple visit from the postman had turned her life around from despair to ecstasy almost.

She picked up the letter once again, still unable to believe that her mind was not playing tricks, and reread it. But it had actually said what was too good to be true. Her father had suddenly come into a large sum of money. He did not elaborate as to how this miracle had happened, but she could only conclude that his abysmal luck had finally changed and he had won at cards. Not a fortune, perhaps. But enough to maintain the two of them in comfort if they practiced a few economies. He planned to buy a house for them in a village outside of Paris. Expenses would be less there, he explained. And as soon as he had done so and made a few other arrangements, he would send for her. He remained her affectionate father, Charles Prior.

She was not fantasizing. Just a week ago she had suffered the humiliation of Lord Gresham's proposition. Now the wheel of fortune had truly borne her to the top. She would no longer have to face the present Lady Blakeney's cool contempt. Or accept the dowager's charity. She should shout, dance, do something to express her joy. But, still, she simply sat there.

Her numb mind moved on to practicalities. She wouldn't speak of this until her father sent the promised ticket for the trip across the channel. Since nothing had been settled definitely, nothing need be done about the school. She felt a sudden pang at the thought of saying good-bye to Emmy. But that would happen in any case. Emmy would make her come-out, would marry. Besides, since money was no problem in that young lady's life, she could visit often in France. No, there was nothing to tie her to this place. No loose ends at all.

The necklace!

Suddenly she remembered her mother's jewelry. She must buy it back at once. Thank goodness she had had no need to part with any of the carefully hoarded sum that she'd received for it.

Andrea hurried to fetch the purse, carefully locked up in her empty jewelry box, and snatched her heavy cloak out of the wardrobe. Pausing only to tell the butler that she had an urgent need of ribbon, she set off at a near run for the village.

She arrived, completely out of breath, at Mr.

Webster's shop and thought at first that the look of dismay on his face came from the fact that he could not understand her.

She took a deep breath and spoke more slowly. "I'd like to buy back my necklace, Mr. Webster. I have the money with me to do so now."

"But I'm afraid that's impossible, Miss Prior." He nervously rearranged a display of buttons on his counter. "You see, I've sold it."

"You've what?" The room was beginning to spin around her. The ringing in her ears prevented her from hearing him correctly.

"Sold it, miss."

"But you cannot have done so."

"Begging your pardon, I'm sure," he sounded injured, "but that is precisely what I am in business to do. Sell things."

"But . . . but I had understood that you would hold it a while for me."

He looked uncomfortable. His words were directed past her left ear, which was as close as he could come to looking at her. "Well, miss, I did hold it a day or so. But seeing as how I had so much of my capital tied up in it, I couldn't afford not to sell it when I had the chance, don't you see."

Andrea did see. Her mother's diamond heart, her last possession left behind, was now irretrievable. Unless . . ." She grasped at a final straw.

"Would you please tell me who bought it, Mr. Webster? Perhaps he—or she—might be persuaded to sell it back to me."

There was a lengthy pause. The storekeeper seemed to be weighing the ethics of the situation. He looked around as though to reconfirm that except for them and a calico cat the shop was empty.

"Well," he at last concluded, "I collect it can do no harm to say as how it was his lordship who bought it."

"You can't mean Lord Blakeney!"

"Well, now, miss," Mr. Webster explained patiently, "Lord Blakeney's the only permanent type of lordship we have in these parts, though I grant you that others do come and go up at the Hall. But if someone around here says 'his lordship,' folk know straight off just who we mean."

"Yes, of course. I see. He would be the one," Andrea said dully as she turned toward the door. "Thank you, Mr. Webster," she remembered to say belatedly as she opened it to go out into the street.

The walk back to the dower house was much more time consuming than the one in the opposite direction had been. Blakeney had her mother's necklace. No, she amended, Blakeney had *purchased* her mother's necklace. The likelihood of its still being in his possession was remote. For, she reasoned, his only need to go to Mr. Webster's establishment to buy a trinket was to find a gift for someone not eligible to receive the Blakeney jewels. She could well imagine his amazement when Mr. Webster produced a necklace of such value. He must certainly place a high value on his mistress to reward her so handsomely. All the joy of the morning had faded. Andrea felt ill at the thought of her mother's diamond heart adorning that lovely wanton.

Still, perhaps it was not too late. Andrea clutched at straws as she walked between the griffin-topped pillars that flanked the entrance to the estate. Perhaps what was done could be undone. Perhaps if she explained, appealed to his better nature, she could still buy the jewel back. It would have no special meaning for his light-o'-love. Surely she would be willing to settle for another just as valuable.

Though she found the prospect distasteful in the extreme, she was determined to let no time elapse before throwing herself on his lordship's mercy. Upon arriving back at the dower house, she went directly to the library and penned a short note, which she bribed a footman to deliver unobserved. She then waited on pins and needles for a reply.

She should have set the meeting place herself, she fumed an hour later as she hurried toward the empty cottage that the dowager intended for her schoolhouse. Still, she admitted to herself, she had stressed that she needed to speak to him in private. This precluded his coming to the dower house and she certainly was not going to call upon him at the Hall. So the choice was, she supposed, sensible. It was just that she did not care for the place's associations. Still, her business would not take long.

He was waiting outside the house, dressed in his five-caped greatcoat and blowing a cloud of smoke from a freshly lit cigar. She felt placed at an unfair disadvantage as he leaned back against the door with a suggestive grin and watched her hurried progress down the farm road and up the cottage path.

"Well met, Miss Prior." The grin widened as she arrived. "I must confess that the last thing I ever expected from life was to be invited to tryst with you. But I was never one to question my luck, just enjoy it."

"Oh, please. Spare me your humor. This is no tryst, as you perfectly well know." She spoke more sharply than she had intended. "Well, at least not in the way you imply," she amended more pleasantly, recalling that it was not politic to be at daggers drawn with a man from whom one wished a favor.

"Blast! You've certainly dashed my hopes," he teased. "Oh, well. *C'est la vie.* Shall we go inside, Miss Prior?" He moved to open the door. "I'm agog to hear why you did wish to see me, if not for, er, romantic reasons."

"I can tell you my business out here just as well. It will only take a minute."

"Suit yourself. But we are in plain view of a well-traveled road. And I'm not the only low-minded person who is likely to misunderstand our assignation."

She could not argue with his logic and preceded him inside, where she came to a halt just beyond the threshold.

"Wouldn't we be more comfortable upstairs where there's a place to, ah, sit?"

She longed to wipe off the perpetual grin that widened as a vision of the dirty feather bed rose before her eyes. "This will do nicely," she answered repressively. "As I just said, I only need a moment of your time."

"Even so, do you mind if I make myself comfortable?" He walked over and sat on the staircase, high enough to look down upon her as he lounged back with his elbows on the higher tread. "I've had a fatiguing day. Climbing out of bed at eleven o'clock undid me. Now what's this pressing business, Andrea?"

"It's about a piece of jewelry you purchased from Mr. Webster in the village. I sold it to him, you see. But with the condition, so I had understood, that he would hold it for a bit and allow me the opportunity to buy it back."

"Well, now, that is amazing. Never realized that our Mr. Webster had turned into a regular pawnbroker."

"Well, he hasn't. That is to say, he sold it at the first opportunity. To you."

"Ah, yes. I do seem to recall. Heart-shaped trinket, was it?"

"It was no *trinket*, sir." Her tone was out of control again. "It was a valuable piece of jewelry left me by my mother."

"I stand corrected."

She tried to be conciliatory. "It's the only thing I had left of hers, you see. And I am most desirous of getting it back. I have the money with me to reimburse you. And I was hoping that you could persuade the young woman you bought it for to allow you to exchange it for some other . . . trinket."

His eyes narrowed. "What makes you think I bought it for a particular person?"

"Well, you would scarcely plan to wear it yourself."

"And now you expect me to go snatch it off this mysterious female's neck?"

"Hardly that. I had thought that if you explained—about the pawning business—and offered a replacement, the . . . person might understand."

"The 'person' you seem to be referring to is not noted for her understanding. She would know a 'trinket's' value down to the last pence, believe me."

Andrea was beginning to feel ill. "I can't pay any more than Mr. Webster paid me for it. But if you'd be willing to wait for the rest . . ."

"No need to look so stricken." He reached into his pocket and pulled out a box. "You're in luck," he said dryly. "Due to its heart shape, I had intended the . . . trinket for a valentine. So here it is, safe and sound." He pulled the necklace from the box and dangled it before her eyes. She almost snatched it from his hand.

"Oh, thank goodness!" Her eyes were moist. "I can't begin to say how relieved . . . I had hated so to part with it. It's the one thing, you see, that Papa didn't . . . Well, never mind. I can never repay you properly, but here is the sum Mr. Webster gave me. I had intended to use it for the school, you see, but now my plans have changed. Because . . ."

"Because your father has suddenly come into a great deal of money."

Her astonishment was evident. "However did you know that? I have not even had time to tell Emmy."

"But you did explain it to Mr. Webster. I collect he thinks some rich relative of yours conveniently departed this vale of tears."

"And he sent you word of it immediately?" Her voice was indignant.

"Naturally. You should know, Andrea, that little around here escapes me. How else did you imagine that I showed up here with your jewelry? You surely can't believe that I go around carrying it next to my heart?"

"I really didn't think. I was too relieved, I collect, to wonder. In any case, here is your money back, Lord Blakeney. And my gratitude." She thrust a handful of bank notes toward him.

"I don't want your blunt."

"You know perfectly well that I can't accept your charity."

"No, I don't suppose you can." He rose from the stairs, took the notes from her hand, and stuffed them in his pocket. "I can accept your gratitude, however." She was caught completely off guard as he took her in his arms and kissed her.

She emerged, after a lengthy interval, gasping and furious. "How dare you make such a habit of this?"

"Oh, come now, Andrea. No need to get in such a taking. You surely must know by now the sort of effect you have on us pathetic, miserable creatures of the opposite sex. Why, look at poor old Gresham. Reduced to making a complete cake of himself. And without a tenth of the exposure to those wide, innocent eyes and inviting lips that I've had."

"Do you know what your problem is, Lord Blakeney?"

"Which one, Miss Prior?"

"Your problem is that with the tiniest bit of effort on your part you could actually be nice. And the fact that you are so close to being so throws a person completely off her guard. It is most unfair!"

She turned and stalked out the door, slamming it behind her and right in his face.

Chapter
Sixteen

*In her fury—whether at Blakeney or herself, she did not stop to consider—*Andrea almost passed the two men without taking any note of them. But when the taller and older of the two cleared his throat and accosted her, "Beg pardon, miss," she recognized the broad-brimmed hat and red vest of the Bow Street Runner.

The spokesman lifted his hat and spoke politely. "We're looking for the cottage of a Mrs. Cannon. Would you happen to know its direction?"

"Why on earth do you wish to see her?" she blurted out.

"That's private business, miss." The short, tubby man was the more officious of the two.

"Oh, is it, indeed?" Andrea hardly recognized the toplofty voice as her own. "Mrs. Cannon is quite
134

elderly and also unwell. I should not like to see her upset. Nor would Lady Blakeney, I can tell you."

"We will certainly do our best not to upset her, miss." The older man spoke placatingly. "Actually, our business ain't with her. We're here to make inquiries about her grandson."

"Zach Cannon?"

"The same."

"Well, then, you'll not object if I come along to show you the way."

The little man was clearly about to do just that when the other intervened smoothly. "Not in the least, miss. We'd take it kindly, in fact. It's good to have an impartial witness in these cases. You'd be amazed at how little respect for the law some of these rural folks can have and how our actions can get misinterpreted in the telling."

As Andrea retraced her footsteps to escort the two Runners, she carefully averted her eyes from the "schoolhouse" when they passed it. Even so, she had the creepy sensation of being watched.

"Let me go in first," she said when they'd reached Mrs. Cannon's cottage.

But this time the senior officer was all business. His conciliatory tone was missing. "You'll wait out by the gate till we call you, miss. There could be a desperate man holed up inside."

Andrea reluctantly agreed to wait, then shouted out in protest as the two burst into the cottage without any warning. Despite what she'd been told, she went running up the pathway after them. Oblivious to the raw draft that swirled and smoked the fire in the fireplace, she stopped short within the doorway to stare at the tableau.

Mrs. Cannon, seated in a chair beside the bed,

which had been shifted near the fireplace, froze in the act of feeding her grandson. The spoon had stopped en route from bowl to mouth. Zachery Cannon, his otherwise bare shoulder and chest swathed in bandages, was propped up by pillows almost in a sitting position against the headboard. His face was as white as the pillows' covering as he gaped at the interlopers looming over him.

The shorter one had produced a pistol and was pointing it at the bedridden man. His companion cleared his throat. "Zachery Cannon, I arrest you in the king's name for robbery and insurrection."

Mrs. Cannon let out a moan and dropped the soup bowl. Its contents spread over the counterpane and onto the floor. Andrea raced to her side and caught her as she slumped sideways in her wooden chair.

"Lower her head, miss," the tall man said matter-of-factly. "I expect she's fainted."

"Get up, you, and get dressed." The short one waved his pistol beneath Zach Cannon's nose.

"Are you out of your mind?" Andrea stormed. "Can't you see he's not able? And how dare you burst in on decent folks this way. You may have frightened Mrs. Cannon to death."

The head lowering seemed to be having an effect, however. Mrs. Cannon raised herself up in her chair and began to keen softly. "Oh, Zach, Zach, what's to do, what's to do."

"I say there." A languid voice spoke in the still open doorway. "What's going on here?"

"Oh, please, do something!" Andrea's voice rose to near hysteria. "These men say they're going to take Mrs. Cannon's grandson. And it's obvious that he should not be moved."

Blakeney sauntered into the room, thoughtfully

closing the door behind him. "It's like the Arctic in here," he observed as he came to stand over the bed beside the Runners. "How are you feeling today, Zach?" he asked politely. He got a look of pure hate for his answer.

"I say." He turned and stared down his nose at the small officer of the law. "Would you put that barker away, man? You're scaring Molly half to death, and if you think Zach here's going to jump you, well, I'd say you give him too much credit.

"Now tell me." He looked at the tall man as the more obviously responsible. "What's this all about?"

"And just who might you be, sir?" The tone was respectful.

"I'm Blakeney."

"Thought you must be. This fellow's one of yours, is he?" He jerked his head toward Cannon. "Well, the fact is, he was one of a group of rioters who broke into Beckwith's shop in London two nights ago and stole a quantity of arms, intending insurrection. One of the guards put a bullet in him, as you see. And we eventually traced him here. We'll be taking him back with us, sir."

"No, I'm afraid you won't be able to do that, Officer." His lordship's voice was filled with regret.

"We've got no choice, sir."

"What he's done's a hanging offense," the officious one chimed in, and Mrs. Cannon gave a soft moan and closed her eyes.

"Keep quiet, you monster!" Andrea hissed.

"As I was saying," Lord Blakeney continued patiently, "I'm afraid you can't take Zach. While I grant you he was born to be hanged, it won't be for your London riot. Fact is, he wasn't there."

"Oh, yes, he was," the small man blustered. "We've got any number of witnesses that put him there, including the fellow who shot him."

"Then you have any number of liars or nobcocks." Blakeney's voice was chilly. He was every inch the lord of the manor as he outstared the Runner. "Fact is, Zach Cannon hasn't been anywhere for the last three days except in this bed. He got a bullet in the shoulder right enough, but your London cove didn't put it there."

"Oh, no? I collect he up and shot himself then, did he?" the small man sneered.

"No, as a matter of fact, he didn't. I did."

There was a stunned silence.

The tall Runner cleared his throat. "Do I understand you to be saying, sir, that you shot this man yourself?"

"That's correct." Blakeney might have been confessing to rabbit hunting.

"I don't believe it." The short one glared.

He was again the recipient of the Blakeney stare.

"Perhaps your lordship would care to explain," the other Runner interjected smoothly. "Out shooting, were you, and hit him by accident?"

"Now that, sir, is insulting." His lordship looked injured as he shifted his gaze to the senior officer. "When I shoot, I hit what I aim for. Don't mind saying I'm noted for my skill. Regular nimrod, in fact."

"Then how?" The Runner jerked a thumb toward the bed.

"No accident, I can tell you."

"You mean to say you meant—"

"Damned right, I did. Didn't mean to kill him, of course. Which you'll observe I didn't do." His lordship smiled around the room, his vaunted marksmanship now vindicated.

"But *why*, sir?"

"Well, now, I don't believe I'd like to go into all of that." He glanced significantly at the two women present.

"I'm afraid we'll have to have an explanation, your lordship. This may all prove to be a bit much for our superiors to swallow."

"Oh, very well then, dammit. The fact of the matter is that he and I had a fight over some wench we both fancied. He couldn't accept the fact that she preferred me over him, don't you see. Tried to put it all down to the lord-of-the-manor business. Droit du seigneur, indeed." He looked disgusted. "Never heard anything so feudal in my life." He looked around the room for vindication but quickly passed over Andrea's shocked face.

"Anyhow, he wouldn't let the thing alone. Jumped me in the dark when I was returning from—well, never mind where—and gave me a pummeling." He touched the almost faded bruise on his face gingerly. "He'd never have gotten away with it, mind you, if the coward hadn't taken me by surprise. Anyhow, I staggered home, got my gun, and came back here and shot him."

"You did what! Sir."

"You heard me," Blakeney said. "But that's quite enough about that. The only thing that concerns you here and now is that this scoundrel was not in London, more's the pity, when your break-in took place and that your man shot someone else there."

"Well, I'm amazed he didn't just let us take the poor sod and 'ang 'im."

The short Runner addressed his remark, sotto

voce, to the ceiling, but Blakeney answered anyhow.

"My God, man, what do you take me for?"

"I shouldn't like to say, m'lord."

"Couldn't let you cart him off for something he didn't do, now, could I? My kind looks after its own. Noblesse oblige and all that sort of thing, don't you know." Again Lord Blakeney looked around him for approval that was not forthcoming.

"Oh, well." He sighed. "At any rate, that finishes your business here. You can get on back to Bow Street now and make your report."

"Let's not be too hasty, your lordship." The tall man walked over to the bed where Zach Cannon had turned his face to the wall during Blakeney's recital. "Would you care to prefer charges, Mr. Cannon? This man has just confessed to shooting you in cold blood. The law's for everyone, you know. Not just the privileged."

Zach Cannon's reply was a contemptuous snort.

"Come, man, this is England."

"What do you mean, 'cold blood,' " his lordship blustered. "It was self-defense. The damned son— the fellow almost killed me. You should have seen me right after the attack. Any number of people did. Wasn't a pretty sight, I can tell you. Self-defense, pure and simple."

"Self-defense? When you've just said you had to go home, get your gun, and come back?" The Runner's voice was scornful.

"Oh, well, now. As to that I could have gotten the details a bit confused after being knocked senseless, don't you know. I expect I must have had my pistol with me. Yes, by Jove, the more I think on it, that's what happened. I had my barker all along." His grin was triumphant.

"I'm sure he could have an even better story by the time a trial took place." Zach Cannon's voice was bitter. "And which of us would your judge and jury believe?"

"And your grandmother here would be turned out of her cottage, I've no doubt." The younger Runner's red vest swelled with indignation.

"What do you think?" There was defeat in the voice from the bed.

The younger man could merely sputter. It was left to his colleague to sum up the situation. "I think, sir, that this is the worst miscarriage of justice I've seen in a lifetime."

Andrea had no words to add. She was far too sick at heart. She could not even bring herself to look at Lord Blakeney. She simply reached over and gave Molly Cannon's hand a squeeze, then hurried from the cottage.

Chapter Seventeen

*S*he would not cry. Of that much she was determined. Nor would she in any way try to sort out her feelings for Blakeney. She had no need to reconcile in her own mind the diversity of character that would allow a man to shed tears over a horse that had to be destroyed and then callously put a bullet into a human being. And over a lightskirt! No, she would not think of it. She had no need to think of it. Thank God, she would soon be joining her father abroad. Lord Blakeney would no longer be a concern of hers. Not that he had ever been.

"Oh, Andrea, there you are," Emmy called from the withdrawing room as she entered the house. "Where have you been? We've been waiting ages. Do come hear the news."

Welcoming a diversion of any kind, Andrea

obeyed the summons. "We" turned out to be Sir Nigel and Mr. Austen, who rose to their feet as she entered. The Beau pulled another chair into the grouping around a tea table.

Emmy filled Andrea's cup from a silver pot and leaned toward her. "We must talk fast before Grandmama returns," she said in a near whisper. Andrea took note of a vacant chair and a half-empty cup. "The bailiff's here on business and they're closeted in the library, but she could return at any moment. What I wish to tell you is that amongst us all we've learned why Lady Blakeney left London in such a high dudgeon."

She looked expectantly at Andrea. Since that young lady could hardly say "Who gives a fig?" she managed a lukewarm "Indeed?"

Emmy was piqued by her reaction. "Well, you won't be quite so uncaring, I assure you, when you discover that you are the main reason her ladyship has descended upon us, quite out of the blue."

"*I'm* the reason!"

Andrea's astonished reaction was everything her friend might have hoped for.

"Oh, but I say, Miss Sedley," Sir Nigel interposed, "calling Miss Prior here the main reason is doing it rather brown, wouldn't you say?"

"He's right, you know." Beau Austen laughed. "Let's give Lord Rathbone first place."

"First, last, what's the difference? Will someone please tell me why I'm involved at all?"

"Because," Emmy said, giggling, "oh, this is too ridiculous. My aunt has rushed home to save her precious son from you."

"Lord Blakeney? From me!" Andrea set her full teacup down with a splash.

"Yes, isn't it hilarious? She has got the notion that Grandmama is throwing you at Blakeney's head."

"But that's disgusting. However did she get such a shatter-brained idea?"

"Oh, I'm sure that one of the servants—Higgens, most likely—keeps her informed of everything that happens. We have no secrets. You must know that. And I'm sure she has decided that the school is just Grandmama's scheme to give you more time to bring Blake to heel."

"Oh, I don't believe any of this for one minute. Why on earth would Lady Blakeney think that the dowager would promote a match between her grandson and me? Why, she would hate the notion fully as much as her daughter-in-law."

"No, actually, she wouldn't," Emmy replied after a thoughtful moment. "For she'd expect you to take her side against her high-and-mighty ladyship. But you are right, of course, the whole thing is merely moonshine. For Grandmama intends for Blake to marry Miss Sanders. Why, her holdings would almost double the estate."

"Oh? Miss Sanders is really that rich?" Beau Austen looked thoughtful.

For whatever reason Emmy chose to ignore his question. "But it doesn't matter whether Lady Blakeney is or is not mistaken in the business," she continued. "For the fact remains that her belief has caused her to produce her own candidate for Blakeney's bride. Her choice is Lady Deborah Wantage."

"Indeed?"

There was a world of difference between Andrea's previously disinterested use of that word and the emotion-choked utterance she gave it this time.

144

Fortunately, Emmy misread the emotion. "Oh, I don't blame you for wishing to laugh. It sent me into whoops, too, I don't mind saying. As if the most sought-after beauty in London would be interested in my clodpole of a cousin."

"Oh, come now," Sir Nigel protested. "Blakeney would be a prime catch for any female. There is the title thing, of course. But in himself he's quite personable, you must admit. And," he added with obvious envy, "tall."

"Not to mention *his* fortune." Beau Austen's expression gave away nothing.

"Well, as far as we're concerned, Lady Deborah's feelings are completely beside the point. The marvelous news is this, Andrea. My aunt is giving a Valentine's ball for the sole purpose of throwing her ladyship at my cousin's rustic head and she is asking everyone for miles around and some from as far away as London. And Mr. Austen and Sir Nigel here have just hand-carried our cards of invitation. Isn't it famous?"

"Oh, yes, indeed." She was falling back on that word again. Strange the way her vocabulary had shrunk since her encounter with the Bow Street Runners. Well, no matter. With any luck at all she could leave for France before the ball took place.

"We were not as altruistic as you might suppose when we offered to deliver your cards," Mr. Austen was saying. "To be truthful, we wished to escape the Hall. You cannot imagine what an uproar this hurry-up ball has caused. Her ladyship is issuing orders a dozen a minute. The servants are beside themselves."

"But we are saving the best piece of scandal for the last, Andrea." Emmy's eyes sparkled with mis-

145

chief. "My aunt did not hurry to Kingswood primarily on her son's account. That is a Banbury tale if ever I heard one. The truth is, she could no longer bear to show her face in London. She has, in fact, become the on-dit of the Season." She paused expectantly.

"Whatever for?" her friend asked, more to be obliging than from interest.

"Well, you do remember that I told you her name has been coupled with Lord Rathbone's for donkey's years? And I did mention, did I not, that his wife obligingly died about a year ago?"

"Really now, Miss Sedley, for shame." Beau Austen shook his head in mock disapproval while he chuckled.

"Well, it *was* obliging of her. At least so everybody thought. Especially my aunt, I'll wager. It only needed a decent interval to lapse after the funeral for him to make an offer. Well, it did and he did. The only thing was"—and here she was convulsed with laughter—"he m-made an offer to a s-schoolroom miss."

"Oh, surely not." Andrea, to her surprise, felt a pang of sympathy for the rejected Lady Blakeney.

"S'truth. His fiancée is younger than we are. We know her, in fact. She was at school, a year behind us. You remember Miss Robinson, do you not?"

Andrea frowned a moment. "Yes, vaguely."

"Oh, 'vaguely' is the only way that one could recall her. She was a mousy little thing. Can you imagine her stealing Lord Rathbone from right under my aunt Blakeney's nose?"

"Doesn't take a lot of imagination, actually," Sir Nigel offered thoughtfully. "She's rich as Croesus.

And it's a known fact that Rathbone's pockets are to let."

"Well, I still think it's excessively amusing that my toplofty aunt should get such a setdown. It certainly explains why she got into such a taking when she saw Blake draw Gresham's cork. I'm sure she was only waiting for a prime excuse to pitch a tantrum of some kind."

"Actually, one has to feel rather sorry for her," Sir Nigel said reflectively. "Though she's still undoubtedly a handsome woman, she has to be fairly long in the tooth. Doesn't look it, though. Wouldn't have dreamed she was Blake's mother. Doesn't look half old enough. But the fact is, she's not likely to get many more chances to drag some cove to the altar. All this must have come as a blow."

"You would not feel the least bit sorry if you'd had to put up with all of her high flights the way Grandmama and I have," Emmy retorted. "Still though"—her face fell a bit—"I must admit that it would be a very good thing if she were to marry *somebody*. Our lives would be much simpler. And she'd no longer have possession of the town house.

"But I refuse to upset myself over that sort of thing just now. For it's all absolutely too famous. Here we were longing for a ball and my meanspirited cousin wouldn't give one and now we're to have one after all. And you may scoff if you wish, Andrea, but I for one am convinced that all those old-fashioned spells we worked have something to do with the fact that this is certain to be the best St. Valentine's Day ever."

Chapter Eighteen

*A*ndrea had spent much of the night wide awake while the events of the past few days whirled in her brain like a kaleidoscope. As a consequence she overslept. When she did open her eyes, it was to the sight of Emmy, still clad in her dressing gown, seated on the floor in front of the fire surrounded by an array of paper, lace, paints, and scissors.

"What on earth?" Andrea rubbed her eyes and refocused them.

"I'm making a valentine." Emmy, intent on coloring a paper heart, did not look up from her work.

"I can see that. But isn't it a bit late?" Andrea slid out from beneath the covers and reached for her own dressing gown. "Today *is* Valentine's Day. Besides, I thought you took care of all that ages ago."

"I thought so, too. But circumstances change."

There was a moment of near silence while Emmy's scissors clicked busily.

"Well?"

"Well what?"

"Aren't you going to explain?"

"Hmmm." Emmy considered the possibility thoughtfully. "No, I collect it might be best that I not do so. I believe I've hit on a marvelous scheme. But things have a way of not turning out as one intends, so perhaps it is best that you don't know. For," she added candidly, "it would be just like you to try to talk me out of this."

"Oh, dear."

"There. See what I mean? Your very tone is dampening even when you don't have the slightest idea of what I'm doing."

"I'm sorry." Andrea switched from dampening to contrite, though instinct told her she might better have stayed with the former.

"Now you must not bother me, for I have to come up with a verse, which is by far the hardest part. Still," she said, brightening, "I should be able to adapt one of the verses I've used before. I don't have time to waste if I'm to beat the postman." She closed her eyes and held her head in her hands to aid creativity.

As the day progressed, it was hard to remain blue-deviled in the face of Emmy's mounting excitement. First there was the business of deciding what to wear that evening. Emmy had a great deal to say about her aunt's unseemly rush that had allowed no one sufficient time to have a new ball gown made. Andrea replied practically that since all the other ladies were in the same situation, it hardly mattered. Besides, since Mr. Austen had not seen any of Emmy's "dreary old gowns," he'd be just as impressed by one of those as he would a new one.

Emmy waived that argument. "That's not the point, silly. Men never really notice what one wears. It's the females one wishes to impress and put at a disadvantage."

"Oh, I see. Well, I do think you might manage that with the Urling's net."

"But I have done so already at the Wakefields' Assembly. One cannot expect to have the same effect twice. No, I think I shall wear the white spotted crape. Only about a half-dozen of the ladies here will have seen it. And what about you, Andrea?"

"Since I have only the one ball gown, there is no problem."

Emmy wrinkled her nose. "You mustn't appear in that old thing. *You* shall wear the Urling's net."

"Indeed I shall not. You've just admitted that that particular gown has lost all its power to put the other ladies at a disadvantage."

"It has never been seen on you, though."

"I cannot believe that matters. No, that gown has definitely lost its magic. Whereas since my British net has merely cast Miss Wadsworth's young ladies into a state of abject envy, it should still be capable of a similar effect on the females of this neighborhood. I shall definitely wear it."

"Goose!"

"*I'm* a goose? After all, it's your theory."

The remainder of the morning was spent eagerly, on Emmy's part at least, awaiting the arrival of the post. When at last it came and Miss Sedley had pounced on the bundle of folded missives and shuffled through it twice, she handed Andrea her share. "It appears that we have each received two valentines. Isn't that nice? There's no need for one of us to be envious of the other." There was a tinge of disappointment in her voice.

Andrea was examining her two and smiled. "Oh, but one of mine is a letter from my father, so I shall take on the proper shade of green."

They returned to their bedchamber to escape the curious eyes of the housemaids. Andrea took her father's letter to the window seat, needing the February light to decipher his hasty scrawl.

As she began to read, a look of consternation replaced her eager anticipation. She was dimly aware of Emmy's oohs and ahs as she opened her valentines. Her friend's running commentary on "cunning Cupids" and "sweet violets" was in ironic contrast to her father's calamitous news.

She read it through again, convinced that she must surely have misunderstood. But there was nothing she had skipped over, no line misread. He had had an abysmal run of luck. The money was all gone. She must try not to think of him too harshly. Nor should she despair. Things were certain to turn about again and he'd be able to send for her in the near future. In the meantime his only consolation came in knowing that she would be happy staying on a bit longer in dear England with her valued friend.

"Which do you think the prettier, Andrea?"

Emmy was forced to ask the question twice before she got her friend's attention. Her two valentines were spread before her on the floor and she was kneeling before them, thoughtfully studying each in its turn.

"They are both lovely." Andrea hoped her answer sounded diplomatic rather than disinterested.

"Yes, they are, are they not? Indeed, they are quite the prettiest I have ever seen. Mr. Austen's is quite the larger, of course."

Andrea then did give the valentines a glance and noted a minuscule difference in their sizes.

"And the bluebirds flying above a temple of love are almost sure to be a declaration. Don't you agree?"

"Oh, indeed." Andrea was on her third heartsick reading.

"But I must say that in all honesty I find the verse quite disappointing."

"Well, everyone can't be a poet." Andrea refolded her father's letter.

"No, but it shows a certain . . . lack of dedication . . . not to at least try." Emmy had picked up Mr. Austen's valentine and was frowning at it. "This poem is from *Valentine Writers*, I'll bet a monkey. I'm sure I've seen it before."

"Well, we regretted not having a copy, did we not? It is the sentiment that counts. After all, he had many to choose from."

"Y-yes. I suppose so." Emmy's tone left room for doubt. "On the other hand"—she discarded the one valentine to pick up the other—"I'm fairly sure— no, I am positive—that Sir Nigel has written his own. Just listen to this:

> "Roses are red,
> Violets are blue.
> When I'm awake
> I think of you.

"Violets are blue,
Roses are red.
I dream of you
When I'm in bed.

"I certainly don't recall anything like that from the *Valentine Writers*, do you?"

Andrea was diverted enough to have to hide a smile. "No, indeed. I have heard nothing like it."

"There! I knew it was an original. Yes, I must say that Sir Nigel's valentine is the superior of the two."

She jumped up and approached the window seat. "But I haven't seen yours. Why, you haven't even opened it."

"No, I had quite forgot. I was too engrossed in Papa's letter."

Emmy gave her a long look. "Is everything all right? Your father isn't ill, is he?"

"Oh, no. Papa is quite well, thank you. It's just that . . . Well, he says that he can't send for me quite as soon as he'd hoped, that's all."

"Good!" Emmy's smile was rallying. "I cannot bear the thought of your leaving and think it's most disloyal of you even to consider it. Now do look at your valentine, for I am dying to do so.

"Ooh," she cooed as the heavy paper was un-folded to display a border of delicately leafed vines entwining hearts and flowers. In the center was a steepled church. "That's quite the prettiest I have ever seen." There was a tinge of envy in her voice. But then she rallied. "However, there's no verse. A valentine should always express a sentiment. Don't you agree?"

"Oh, yes, indeed." Andrea's mind had returned

to the money that her father had lost. It was rapidly assuming the status of a fortune in her thoughts.

"Even a secondhand verse is better than no verse at all. Don't you agree?"

"Oh, yes."

Emmy was peering more closely at the flawed valentine. "Why, there's no signature, either. Who do you suppose? Andrea!"

"I beg pardon, what did you say?" Andrea snapped out of her painful reverie.

"Your valentine's not signed. Who do you think sent it?"

"Papa."

"Oh, it's from your father then. I had thought perhaps . . . Well, never mind. But why did he not sign it?"

"I expect he simply forgot." Andrea picked up the pretty card and gazed at it sadly. "Papa is inclined to be rather . . . careless . . . in some respects."

Chapter
Nineteen

*L*ady Blakeney had worked a transformation. It was apparent when Andrea and Emmy joined the throng collected in the great hall waiting to ascend to the ballroom. Mirrors sparkled. The checkered squares of the marble floor fairly gleamed. The recessed statuary were devoid of cobwebs. Even the suit of armor that lurked in its darkened corner had been burnished.

But no transformation the baroness had wrought could compare to the change in her son. He stood with her at the top of the grand staircase, formally receiving their guests.

"Good heavens!" Emmy breathed in Andrea's ear. "Would you look at Blakeney? I would not have thought it possible. He looks like . . . someone else. If he were not my odious cousin, I would think him handsome."

Andrea, not hampered by kinship, conceded the point. She was accustomed to a carelessly dressed— one might even go so far as to say slovenly dressed— care-for-nothing. This paragon might even have cast the great Beau Brummell in the shade. He was wearing a black velvet long-tailed coat that appeared to be molded to his broad shoulders. His satin knee breeches were of the same color. His stiff shirt points, cravat, and stockings were white, pristine in contrast. His black pumps gleamed, as did the golden signet ring and the watch fob that he wore.

"My aunt must have held a pistol to his head to get such results," Emmy whispered.

"I rather doubt that was necessary," Andrea replied dryly. She had looked beyond his lordship to the beauty he was now presenting to the couple just ahead.

Lady Deborah Wantage was even more lovely than she had been painted: dark-haired, dark-eyed, a statuesque beauty. She appeared very little older than Andrea and Emmy, but her look of sophistication, enhanced by a dark red tunic with a gold-key border worn over a white crape gown, made Andrea feel gauche and provincial in the extreme. She experienced a stab of some other emotion that she refused to identify. For she certainly was not jealous of the beauty in the least. If Lady Deborah wished to cast her lures at a libertine with no shred of conscience, then it only went to prove that some females would go to any lengths to secure a title. She only hoped the beauty had at least an inkling of the kind of man she was dealing with. Still, it was none of her affair.

Lady Blakeney's greeting was decidedly chilly.

This set the tone for Andrea's own reply to his lordship's salutation. It was fully as frigid, if not even more so. His brows rose in mock dismay as he presented the two girls, in tandem, to the honored guest.

"Well," Emmy confided as they passed into a dazzling ballroom that reflected the light of innumerable candles from gold-framed mirrors and crystal prisms. "I suppose I'd rather have her as mistress here than that platter-faced Miss Sanders."

"Aren't you rushing things a bit? Lady Deborah and your cousin have barely met. You sound as if their betrothal was inevitable."

"Isn't it, given her looks and my aunt's determination? Don't you agree?"

The orchestra began to tune up in the musicians' gallery just above their heads. The noise preempted Andrea's reply. She hurried after Emmy, who was determined to find two places together for them on the gilt chairs lining the ballroom walls. These were rapidly being filled by other young ladies who were trying their best to appear indifferent to the fact that in the next few minutes their fates would lie in the balance. They would be asked to take the floor for the first dance or be left to languish with fixed smiles and simulated interest in the sets' performance as if their intent all along had been to observe.

The orchestra had achieved its goal of harmony. Lady Deborah took Lord Blakeney's arm. They would, of course, lead off the dance. Andrea felt Emmy stiffen and followed her narrowed gaze across the ballroom floor. Mr. Beau Austen was making his bow in front of a simpering Miss Sanders.

Before Emmy could comment on this perfidy, Sir Nigel was bowing low before her while he stammered out an invitation to join the set. The smile he received was staggering as Emmy gratefully took his arm.

Andrea seized the opportunity to beat a strategic retreat as she spied a determined-looking middle-aged gentleman heading her way. She chose another chair, as far removed as possible from the orchestra, which was causing an incipient headache to become full-blown. The location had a second advantage. The chair was partially hidden by a giant fern. She intended to observe the dancing for a bit, then slip away unnoticed.

Andrea carefully avoided watching the set where Lady Deborah and Lord Blakeney were the head couple. She scanned the floor looking for Emmy and Sir Nigel and found them next to Lady Blakeney. Her ladyship was partnered by a short, balding gentleman whose girth seemed to have outstripped his evening coat, which strained perilously against its buttons. But if the gentleman's general appearance fell considerably beneath prepossessing, he compensated with a beaming, almost proprietary smile that lit his countenance as he gazed up at the mature beauty beside him. Lady Blakeney, in her turn, appeared totally captivated by her roly-poly partner. Such coquettishness would be second nature to a practiced flirt, was Andrea's cynical opinion.

She closed her eyes to see if this might help her headache and allowed the music to wash over her. From this distance it had become quite soothing. She concentrated on thinking of nothing at all, willing her turbulent mind to become a blank. It refused to cooperate. She switched it back to her schooldays and tried to remember the name of the old-maidish dancing master who had come once a week to give the young ladies instruction. The music began to have a soporific effect. She nodded.

"I see we're keeping you up, Miss Prior."

Her head snapped up and the two Lord Blakeneys looming over her merged into one.

"I was not asleep."

"No, of course not. Had a bad night last night, did you?"

"No. Indeed not. There was no reason for *my* sleep to be disturbed by conscience."

"That's good to know. Still, it does not account for the fact that you look like the very devil."

"Well, thank you very much for that observation. It's precisely what every young lady at a ball would wish to hear. But I refuse to allow my spirits to be lowered by your tactless observation. I am convinced that I look just as I always have. It's only that you are now judging me by a new standard." She nodded in the direction of Lady Deborah, who was being led into a dance by Mr. Austen. "I expect that all of us females look like antidotes when compared to your nonpareil."

He grinned. "Do I possibly detect a note of jealousy in your voice?"

"You do not."

"Oh, well. I collect it's futile to expect the perfect Miss Prior to display an unworthy emotion."

"Never mind. You have enough unworthy emotions for us both."

"Touché. But put away your rapier. I'm here to ask you to stand up with me."

"Thank you very much, Lord Blakeney, but I am not dancing this evening."

"Not at all or only not with me?"

"I cannot see that the distinction matters."

"You are right, as usual. The question is purely academic since I, too, have no desire to dance. I merely extended the invitation as an excuse to talk to you. Actually, this will be much better." He sat down in the chair beside her.

"Lord Blakeney," she seethed, "I do not wish to talk."

"I'll grant you this is not the ideal place for a tête-à-tête. Still, your fern does a fair job of concealment. I had the devil of a time finding you. So if you'll scoot over just a bit more, you should be almost totally hidden. And I shall appear to be talking to myself. That should raise a few eyebrows. But, then, perhaps not."

"Lord Blakeney, I do not seem to have made myself clear. I do not wish to talk to *you*. Not here. Not anywhere. Not ever."

"No? That's unfortunate. For I don't see much you can do about it except get up and walk across the ballroom in a high dudgeon. Which could affect those eyebrows I mentioned even more than an apparent soliloquy on my part."

"So on the whole, I think it might be less painful for you to answer a few brief questions. First, how did you like the valentine I sent you?"

"*You* sent me a valentine? I'll not believe it."

"Of course I did. Wasn't it obvious?"

"Hardly. The only valentine I received bore no signature."

"Oh, should I have signed it? Well now, since you failed to sign the one that you sent me, I decided that must be the latest fashion." He grinned wryly at her embarrassment. "Besides, I thought the Church picture was a dead giveaway. But never mind all that. Here is question number two, why have you been crying?"

"Crying? Really, you do have some nodcock notions. Why should you think that I have been crying?"

"Red eyes? Puffy lids? A nose that glows? Of course, you could always be sickening for something."

"If so, I can only hope it is something contagious."

"You know"—he appeared to look at her with new interest—"I'm certainly seeing a different side of you, Andrea. I'd no notion you could be so waspish. I can remember when you first came here with Emmy and you were no more than . . . What? Eight? Nine? You were wearing a white dress as I recall and you looked to me like some kind of snow maiden from a picture book. Totally aloof. Above the fray. Especially contemptuous of scruffy boys. You looked at me as if I'd crawled out from underneath some dank, mossy stone. I quite longed to fling mud all over that pristine whiteness. To bring you down to earth as it were."

"As I remember you from those days, you probably did. But is there any point to this conversation?"

"Why, yes. I asked why the snow maiden had been crying."

"And I tried to suggest that it was none of your affair. For if you are supposing it had anything to do with—anything at all connected with you, I can assure you, you much mistake the matter."

"I can't tell you how relieved that makes me." There was only the merest hint of sarcasm in his tone.

An uncomfortable silence followed. In search of a distraction from the disturbing presence beside her, Andrea peered between the fronds of the giant fern. Beau Austen, with the beauteous Lady Deborah in his arms, waltzed into view. It took a moment for something that had been niggling at her brain to become apparent. "That's odd," she murmured.

"What's odd?"

"Oh, nothing."

"Come on, Fern, speak up. Or would you rather waltz with me? There's still time for a few twirls around the floor."

"Is that a threat? Well, never mind. I don't mind telling you that I think it's very odd that Mr. Austen has let two dances go by without asking Emmy to be his partner."

"I disagree. There's nothing odd about it. I expect the scales fell from his eyes, that's all."

Something in his tone made her turn and stare at him suspiciously. "Why, I do believe you've warned him off."

"*Warned* him off? Certainly not. Wasn't necessary. I just let slip a few home truths, that's all."

"What sort of truths?"

"Simply that Emmy doesn't inherit her fortune automatically upon marriage. Without my approval, she won't get it until she's twenty-five. Lucy Sanders, on the other hand, is already possessed of a sizable inheritance from her mother. That, coupled with all the squire will eventually leave her, makes my cousin look like a pauper." He chuckled. "Ergo, Beau's charm is now redirected. Not only has he stood up with Miss Sanders for the first dance, I'll bet a monkey he's already settled on a second one and supper."

Her look should have wilted the fern. "I thought he was your friend."

"Oh, he is. We go back years. That's how I've come to know him so well."

"I'll not believe his regard for Emmy was so mercenary."

"Then you're a gudgeon," he replied pleasantly. "I'll not believe you didn't find it wonderful that he cooled off you so quickly."

"There was nothing to wonder about. He simply preferred Emmy."

"Oh, come now. You can't be that lacking in conceit. No man in his right mind would 'simply prefer' Emmy over you. He 'simply preferred' her prospects. Or he did until I dashed them down a bit. No, I hate to disillusion you, but Beau's forced to dangle after a rich wife. Especially after he cut his ties with Gresham."

"I don't see what that odious man has to say to any of this."

"Just that he was keeping Beau in funds. Why else would anyone put up with that bumptious ass?"

"Do you know," she said hotly, "I don't believe any of this. I think you judge everyone by your own shabby standards."

His smile was a bit twisted. "Sorry if I upset your romantic notions. But you did bring up the subject."

"It's not my 'romantic notions' that are in question here. It's your cousin's happiness."

"And you think Beau would assure that? It's just

163

as I thought. You are a devilish poor judge of character, Miss Prior."

"But if they love each other, who are you to stand in the way? You could give your permission and all would be right and tight. He wouldn't need to look elsewhere."

"Men like Beau Austen will always look elsewhere."

"Well, I certainly yield to your expertise on that sort of thing."

"I rather thought you might. But as far as loving each other goes, they don't. Oh, I grant you, Emmy was bedazzled when they first met, but I think she was already cooling off quite a bit. Of course becoming a 'woman scorned' may put her in a taking for a while, God help us, but she'll soon get over it. And then there's always Nigel, who really does love her, for his sins. Wouldn't surprise me at all if they make a match of it after her come-out."

"And you'd approve?"

"Oh, naturally, I'd try to warn the poor sapskull off." He grinned wickedly. "Give him some idea of the life he's letting himself in for. But I doubt it would do any good. He's well and truly smitten."

The music ceased and the dancers were leaving the floor. "Would you care to join the next set, Miss Prior?" he asked politely.

"I've already told you that I've no intention of dancing with you, Lord Blakeney."

"Just as well. I've never cared for dancing above half. Much rather sit here and talk."

She looked horrified. "But you mustn't. People will certainly remark upon it if you remain here. Indeed, if they have not done so already."

"Well, I was never one to begrudge my neighbors

a bit of sport, but I think you misjudge the matter." His eyes narrowed as he gazed across the room. "I think there are other things far more interesting than us to occupy the gossipmongers."

She parted the fern to follow his gaze. The rotund little man was once more making his bow before Lady Blakeney.

"Who is he?" she asked curiously before she remembered her objective was to put a period to their conversation.

"Squire Sanders. Lucy's father. My God, would you watch her? She's almost simpering at that old quiz. I'd no idea she was so desperate."

"I suppose you're going to tell me that *he's* a fortune hunter."

"No, the other way around. But, thank God, it's no concern of mine. They're both of age. And then some."

He was watching the sets form with no apparent intention of leaving.

"Go dance with someone," she hissed. "You're the host here, remember?"

"Oh, I asked and was turned down. That disposes of my duty. Not to mention my pride. A cove has a right to lick his wounds a bit. By the by, why aren't you wearing your mother's necklace? That gown could use a bit of adornment."

"You really are trying to make me feel as great a dowd as possible, aren't you?"

He pondered the question a moment and then grinned his taunting grin. "Damme, you could just be right. It could be that white dress thing all over again." He paused. "But I am surprised that you aren't wearing the necklace. I have a rather proprietary interest in it, you understand."

"Yes, I expect you would have." A thought struck her. "Oh, I say. You wouldn't perhaps care to buy it back?"

"Buy it back? Surely you're funning. Why, I've never seen anyone so glad to be reunited with stone and metal. I'd much liefer rob my own grandmother than buy it back. I say, this is a joke, isn't it?"

"No, it isn't. My circumstances have changed. Again. And I don't think I can any longer be governed by sentimentality," Andrea said. "Of course, I can see that your circumstances have changed as well. You would not now wish it for the same person."

"And which person was that? It slips my mind."

She ignored the question.

"I do not enjoy haggling like a peddler with goods to sell, your lordship. But I might point out that my necklace would make a perfect betrothal present."

"Because of its heart shape? Yes, I expect it would. But why should that interest me?"

"Oh, come now. Everyone knows that you are to become engaged at any time. Why else would Lady Deborah be here?"

"God knows. The country air?"

"I beg pardon. Now it's your turn to tell me that this is none of my affair."

"Wouldn't dream of being so rag-mannered. But I am intrigued by the fact that you think I'll soon be wed. Aren't you rushing things a bit?"

"You're the one who should be rushing. It's my opinion that you should offer for Lady Deborah as soon as possible. Before . . ."

"Oh? Before what?"

166

"Before she finds out too much about you."

"Such as?"

"Such as shooting a man down in cold blood over a . . . over a—"

"Doxy?"

"Whatever."

"And do you, my perfect Miss Prior, intend to tell her?"

"Of course not."

"Whyever not? I should think you'd consider it your Christian duty not to allow an innocent young virgin to become leg-shackled to an unprincipled scoundrel like myself."

"It's certainly not my place to tell her. Besides . . ."

"Oh, please, don't turn shy at this point. Besides what?"

The music had stopped playing and the sets on the dance floor were breaking up.

"She would not believe that such a thing was possible. I mean that you could behave so . . . despicably. Why, I have known you for all these years and I can scarcely credit the thing myself."

"Oh, no?" He rose to his feet and stared down at her, his face a mask. "Now that is a blatant falsehood, Miss Prior. The truth is, is it not, that where I'm concerned, there is nothing too despicable for you to believe."

He bowed perfunctorily and left her staring after him.

Chapter
Twenty

The moon was full and bright. There would be no need for any of Lord Blakeney's guests to stay the entire night if they did not wish to do so. Not that there was any likelihood of the party breaking up before sunrise, Andrea thought as she pulled her cloak tighter against the cold and hurried down the carriage road toward the dower house.

Her headache had worsened as the evening progressed. She had decided that the prudent thing would be to slip away unnoticed and seek the comfort of her bed. The fact that Lord Blakeney had taken the floor for the second time with the beautiful Lady Deborah had nothing whatsoever to do with the increased pounding in her temples. Perhaps a dose of laudanum when she got home. She made it a point, as a rule, to eschew such remedies, but these circumstances were unusual, to say the least.

She had resisted Higgens's insistence that he send for her carriage, explaining that a brisk walk in the fresh air was the very thing she needed. Perhaps that was true as far as her head went. As for her feet, she longed to trade her thin dancing slippers for a pair of stout half boots.

To take her mind off her icy-cold feet, she tried to face her problems squarely as she hurried along. This was not as difficult as she might have imagined. The mysterious part of her mind that produced dreams and such must have been at work without her awareness. For now she saw clearly that she had no options. There was only one course of action open to her. And why she had ever considered the dowager's suggestion of starting a school here on the estate was beyond her.

Andrea slipped quietly into the front hall, hoping not to rouse the servants. That hope was short-lived. It seemed the entire household was still astir. Andrea's heart sank as Lady Blakeney's maid informed her that her mistress was waiting up and had asked to see the young ladies as soon as they came home.

"Come stand by the fire," the dowager barked as Andrea reluctantly entered her bedchamber. The old lady was seated next to the hearth and clad in her nightgown, nightcap, and woolen dressing gown. "Didn't hear a carriage. Don't tell me you walked at this hour of the night and in evening dress. Have you taken leave of your senses? And where is Emeline?"

As she obediently positioned herself as near to the crackling flames as caution would allow, Andrea explained that she was not feeling well and had left the party early. "Emmy probably won't be home for hours," she finished.

"Having a good time then, is she?"

"Why, yes. Certainly. It's a marvelous ball."

There must have been a lack of conviction in her voice, which produced a decided "Humph" from the dowager. But "We'll have some port" was her only comment. "Best thing in the world for the headache."

After the abigail had poured wine into two crystal goblets and served her mistress and Andrea, who was now warm enough to sink into an armchair pulled, like the dowager's, close to the hearth, she gratefully obeyed her ladyship's command to go to bed. "Now we shall have a comfortable cose," Lady Blakeney said to a partially revived Andrea. "I wish to hear all about That Woman's ball. Tell me, did Mr. Austen stand up first with my granddaughter?"

"Well, no, ma'am. Actually, I believe he danced first with Miss Sanders."

"Wind blowing that way, is it?" The dowager didn't look too surprised as she took a long draught of her port. "And I collect that young sprig of a baronet did stand up with Emmy?" She nodded, almost with satisfaction, when Andrea verified that that was indeed the case.

"Now then. What about the London chit that That Woman is throwing at my grandson's head? A beauty, is she?"

Trying to keep her voice from betraying any real interest in the subject, Andrea informed her ladyship that Lady Deborah was indeed a nonpareil.

"Dance a lot with her, did he?"

Andrea replied that Lord Blakeney and Lady Deborah had opened the ball. "As to what happened between them after that, I really couldn't say," she prevaricated.

"Humph" was the noncommittal answer.

"Now then." The Dowager Lady Blakeney inched forward in her chair and fastened Andrea with gimlet eyes. "Tell me about That Woman. Who were her partners? I assume that she did dance. It would not be at all like her to play the matron."

"Well, there again I cannot speak for later on, but I did see her dance the first set with Squire Sanders."

"Did she, b'gad." The old lady cackled delightedly and slapped her knee. "How did the old cod's head act with her?"

"Oh, I should think he was quite smitten."

"Smitten, was he?" Andrea had never seen the dour dowager look so delighted. "And what about That Woman? How did she seem?"

Andrea caught herself just in time before sharing her own conclusion that flirtation was reflex with her ladyship. Instead she observed more tactfully, "She appeared to be enjoying his attention."

"After having just been jilted for a green girl half her age, I wager she was." The other chuckled. "I knew she would be ripe for the plucking."

"You knew?" Andrea looked at her hostess suspiciously.

"That is why I sent that cawker of a squire a sugary valentine and signed her name to it. His wife has been dead for nearly two years now. So he should be good and ready to re-wive. Mark my words, child. That Woman will be out of Kingswood Hall in three months' time or I am not an Englishwoman." She poured herself another brimming glass of port. "Drink up, girl." She frowned at Andrea's untouched glass. "Best thing in the world for the headache, I told you."

Andrea took an obedient sip, hoping it might give her courage. "Lady Blakeney," she blurted out, "there is a favor I wish to ask of you."

"Indeed?" The sharp gaze did little for Andrea's confidence.

"I was wondering if you might buy my mother's necklace from me. You may recall that you remarked on it when I first came here."

"Hmmm. Yes. The heart-shaped thing. Diamonds and a ruby, was it not?"

Andrea nodded.

"But why would you wish to sell it? Think you would want to keep it to remember your dear mother by." The dowager frowned in disapproval.

"I have to have some capital, you see." The words came tumbling out. She needed to buy her passage to France and have money left over to support herself and her father until she could gather a few pupils together.

"Your father is up the River Tick again, is he? Well, you must know by now that he will always be there. And your being with him will not change that."

"I do know. But he still needs me. And," she choked, "I need him."

"I see. Thought we had settled your future. A school here would do quite well, you know." She didn't add "with my patronage," but the words hung in the air anyway.

"I know. And I'm eternally grateful to you for the suggestion. But the more I've thought on it, the clearer it's become that I can't stay here."

The dowager's eyes were boring through Andrea's head. She wished she'd say something. Even "Humph" would be better than this speaking silence. "My father really does need me," she said once more.

"I see."

The terrible part was, Andrea thought, that the Dowager Lady Blakeney most likely did see.

"Well, go to bed, child, and we will talk about it tomorrow. *Today,* I should say. Who knows, you may look at the thing quite differently after a bit of sleep. But if not, of course I will buy your necklace."

Andrea had feared it would be impossible to sleep. But she had just achieved that blessed state when she was roused by a whisper whose volume almost placed it in another category entirely. "Andrea, are you awake?"

"Ummmm. Ah. Yes."

Emmy was leaning over her anxiously while her young maid waited in the background. "Are you all right? I've been quite worried."

Since daylight was beginning to edge between the curtains, Andrea did not think her friend had suffered from an excess of anxiety. "I'm all right. It's only a headache—which a few hours' sleep will cure," she added pointedly.

"Well, you certainly did not miss a thing by leaving the ball early. I've never seen such a tedious affair."

It was obvious that Emmy was bursting to talk. Andrea repressed a sigh and sat up in bed, pulling the covers up around her shoulders as she leaned back against the headboard. "Indeed? I had the impression before I left that most people were enjoying themselves. Still, things may have taken a turn for the worse afterward."

"Oh, *some* enjoyed themselves." Emmy's voice was muffled as the maid pulled her evening gown over her head. "*Some* even went so far as to make complete cakes of themselves."

"Oh, indeed?"

"No need to sound so noncommittal." Emmy hurried into her nightgown and climbed into bed. She waited until the maid had tidied up and left, then said, "You're surely not going to pretend that you did not watch Beau Austen dangle after that platter-faced Lucy Sanders all evening?"

"Well, I did see him stand up with her" was Andrea's diplomatic reply.

"Not only did they dance the first dance together, he stood up with her again for the cotillion and took her in to supper."

"Indeed?"

"For heaven's sake, Andrea, is 'indeed' all you can say?"

"I could switch to 'really' if you think it better. But the truth is, words fail me."

"Well, they should. For I've never experienced such treachery."

"Treachery?"

"Oh, really, Andrea. Turning into an echo is not helping anything. You might just as well go back to 'indeed.'"

"Not actually, for I am not simply filling your pauses now, Emmy. How can you term Mr. Austen's pursuit of Miss Sanders treachery? Poor taste, perhaps, but treachery?"

"It *is* treachery. He was practically fawning over the two of us earlier."

174

"I don't know about the two of us. But, yes, he did show you particular attention. I collect that is his way. To flit from flower to flower, as it were."

"And land in a cow pile?"

"Emmy!" But Andrea laughed in spite of herself. "That's a dreadful thing to say about inoffensive Lucy Sanders. It is not her fault that Mr. Austen seems to be one of nature's flirts."

"What he is," Emmy said with a sniff, "is one of nature's fortune hunters. I tried to quiz Sir Nigel on the subject, but he is far too honorable to gossip about a friend. Even so, I got the distinct impression that the Beau's pockets are to let. And later on Lady Deborah confirmed it for me. She says it's a well-known fact that Mr. Austen is on the prowl for a rich wife. Why, I don't doubt but that accounted, in a small part at any rate, for his interest in me. And Lucinda Sanders, as you know, is a regular moneybags. And I am sure he'll find her a far easier conquest. For I don't mind saying that Mr. Austen's charm was beginning to wear a bit thin. Did you not think him rather too encroaching in his address?"

But Andrea's attention was focused elsewhere. "You and Lady Deborah had a coze?" she asked.

"Why, yes. We ate our supper together. And while Blake and Sir Nigel were filling our plates, I grasped the opportunity to inquire whether she is acquainted with Mr. Austen. It really caused the scales to fall from my eyes when she disclosed that society considers him a here-and-thereian."

Andrea had heard quite enough about Beau Austen. "What did you think of her, Emmy?"

"About Lady Deborah? Well"—she sighed—

"there is no doubt that she quite casts other females in the shade."

"Yes, but aside from that, what did you think of her?"

"What do you mean 'aside from that'? There is no 'aside from that.' When a lady is that dazzling she does not need anything else. At least so far as the male sex is concerned."

"No, I collect not. Still, you must have formed some opinion."

"Well," Emmy said thoughtfully, "it is difficult to really like a person when she causes you to wonder if your complexion looks sallow by comparison and if your hair has stayed in curl. Still, all in all, she seemed quite nice. Too nice by half for my odious cousin. And she certainly feels just as she should about Mr. Austen."

"And is he smitten?"

"By Lady Deborah? Of course not. *She* is not rich. Weren't you attending to anything I've said? I thought I'd made it plain that our Beau"—her lip curled—"spent the entire evening dangling after Miss Sanders."

"I was not referring to Mr. Austen. I meant to say, did Lord Blakeney appear smitten by Lady Deborah?"

"Oh, who can tell about him." Emmy was obviously disinterested. "He was certainly better behaved than usual. Quite the gentleman, in fact. I do believe he did not say one provoking thing to me all during supper. I expect that that in itself indicates something."

"Yes, I expect that it does."

"Well"—Emmy yawned prodigiously—"I will get an opportunity to become better acquainted later today, for my aunt has asked me to drink tea with her and Lady Deborah.

"By the by, I hope you won't mind that you were not included in the invitation. When I suggested that I bring you, Aunt said that we should leave that till another time. Right now she would prefer that Lady Deborah become well acquainted with the family."

"I see."

"No, I don't think you really do. For, absurd as it sounds, I do believe that my aunt considers you Lady Deborah's rival."

"How absurd."

"That's what I just said. But even so, I am convinced that she believes you have your cap set for Blakeney."

Andrea sniffed indignantly. "Well, she need concern herself no longer. For I am leaving tomorrow."

Emmy, who had just prepared for sleep by rolling over on her stomach, did a complete flip-flop to stare at her friend. "You are *what*?"

"Leaving tomorrow. For France."

"But isn't this terribly sudden? I expected you to stay for weeks yet. And what about Grandmama's plans to start a school?"

"That was most kind of her ladyship. But I don't think it would really suit me. I believe I shall have more success teaching English to French children rather than the other way around. Besides, Papa does need me, you know."

"I see."

For the first time Andrea noticed a decided resemblance between grandmother and granddaughter. Emmy was staring at her thoughtfully with much the same expression the dowager had exhibited earlier. "Well, I do wish you would not go. But if your mind is quite made up . . . Right now I think we had best go to sleep."

Andrea could not help but feel a trifle hurt at her friend's rather cavalier dismissal of her news. She was, therefore, pleased when after an interval of rhythmical breathing Emmy whispered, "Andrea, are you still awake?"

"Yes."

"Good. There is something more I wished to say."

"Indeed?"

"Yes, indeed," the other mocked. "I forgot to tell you that one good thing did happen at the ball."

"Oh? And what was that?"

"Squire Sanders and my aunt. The old fool was in hot pursuit of her for the entire evening. And she did nothing to dampen his attention. In fact, she encouraged it. So thanks to me, I'll bet a monkey that her ladyship will be out of Kingswood and presiding over the squire's hall in six months' time."

"Why, thanks to you, pray tell?"

"Because"—Emmy gurgled—"I sent the old sapskull a romantic valentine and signed her name to it, that's why."

Andrea almost blurted out, You, too! Instead she managed to switch her retort to "How Machiavellian."

"How *what*? Well, never mind. We must get some sleep or else look too hagridden for words. Good night, Andrea."

"Good night."

Except it wasn't. It was now clearly morning. And only one good thing could be said about it. At least St. Valentine's Day was now a thing of the past.

Chapter
Twenty-one

After a flurry of packing, Andrea took advantage of Emmy's tea engagement and the dowager's philanthropic visit to a tenant to retire to the library and write her father. Whether he would welcome her change of plans was a moot point that she refused to consider.

She was struggling with how best to break the news when an altercation in the hallway distracted her. She jumped up from the table and ran to the door to listen.

"You've got no business coming here at all, Zach Cannon." Lady Blakeney's majordomo was at his starchiest. "But if you do expect to see any resident of this household, you'll mind your place. Go to the back door and make your request. I shall then decide whether to inquire if the young lady will see you."

"And should I also bow and scrape and pull my forelock?" The other spoke with deep sarcasm.

"It would not come amiss."

"The devil it wouldn't. I don't use back doors, old man, and neither should you. We're as good as the next person and you'd do well to remember it."

"And you would do well not to get ideas above your station."

"My station? Who but God's to say what that is? Certainly not the likes of the lords of Kingswood. But I've no time to talk politics with you, Mr. Brown. Now do you announce me to Miss Prior or do I move you aside and call her myself?"

"There is another possibility. Do I call Frederick and Samuel and have you thrown out?"

Andrea felt it high time to interfere. She hurried toward the open door, where the old man and the young one stood toe to toe glaring at each other, oblivious to the icy blasts that were rapidly lowering the house's temperature. "It's all right, Brown. I shall see Mr. Cannon," she said firmly.

"Her ladyship will not be pleased, miss." The butler's demeanor radiated his own disapproval as he stepped aside to allow the other to enter. As the young man struggled painfully out of his greatcoat, Brown pointedly turned his back. With a wry grin the visitor placed it and his high-crowned beaver on a hall chair, then followed Andrea into the library.

"I am glad to see that you are well enough to be out, Mr. Cannon," she said formally, and indicated a chair near the fire. "Do please have a seat."

"No need for that." Despite all his democratic protestations, Zach Cannon looked uncomfortable. "What I've come to say will only take a minute."

The words seemed to stick in his throat, however.

And he appeared reluctant to meet her eyes as they stood a few feet apart in the center of the Aubusson carpet that filled the room. Finally he said, "I understand you'll soon be leaving here, Miss Prior."

"That's right. I leave tomorrow to join my father in France."

"I see. Well, I'm leaving England, too. I'm on my way right now, as a matter of fact."

"For France?" Andrea began to speculate that the motive for this odd visit was a request to share the carriage that her ladyship would be providing for her journey to Dover.

"No. No, I'm off for America. It's a new country where one man's as good as another. Or so they say."

"I see. Well, then. Good luck and Godspeed, Mr. Cannon."

She did not actually say, What does any of this have to do with me, but her puzzled expression seemed to convey the message. He shifted his feet and came to the point.

"I didn't feel I should leave, though, without clearing up a certain misunderstanding. For I doubt that *he*"—his lip curled a bit—"will condescend to do so."

"What misunderstanding, Mr. Cannon?"

"Well, you were there, Miss Prior, when the Runners came for me. The truth is, they had the right of it, you see. I *was* shot in London where some of us were trying to arm ourselves." He paused to let the words sink in.

"Then Blake . . . Lord Blakeney did not . . . ?"

"No."

"Oh."

Andrea could feel the blood rushing to her face. "It was all . . . You mean the things he said . . .

About the fight over a . . . a woman . . . was all just a tarradiddle?"

"Oh, the fight part was true enough, me thrashing him and all. But the business about going back to fetch a gun and shooting me, that was a lie. And since you, like those Bow Street Runners, seemed to swallow the story, I thought it only right to stop by and set you straight."

"And damned decent it was of you, Zach."

Both parties started and turned toward the door. They had been much too absorbed to hear Lord Blakeney enter. He now stood, arms folded, watching them intently. He was dressed in what appeared to be a brand-new coat of blue superfine. But Andrea was too rattled by the mocking look he gave her to properly appreciate his sartorial splendor.

"But you couldn't quite force yourself to tell a straight story, could you, old fellow? I overheard that bit about thrashing me. Fustian! Next you'll be saying that Boney beat Wellington at Waterloo."

"You'll not deny that in all our fights down through the years I gave at least as good as I got?"

"Now and then, possibly" was the grudging reply. But then his lordship suddenly flashed his impudent grin. "Oh, very well then, dammit. Since they tell me you're leaving, I'll call it a draw. Satisfied?"

To Andrea's amazement, the other man grinned back. The smile transformed his malcontented face to a handsome one. "You know deuced well, Hadrian Augustus Blakeney, that I'll never be satisfied till I rub your aristocratic face in the dirt."

"At least that beats having my head on a pike, which I always believed was your true ambition. But are you sure America's the place for you, Zach? They've already had their revolution, you know."

"I know. But there's no hope for change here. You've seen to that." His expression clouded over once again.

"I'd like to think so. I'd also like to think that a bullet so near the heart cooled your radical tendencies. But I'll not count on that possibility. Oh, by the by." Blakeney reached inside his coat. "I've a farewell present for you."

"No, by God!" the other clenched his fists and took a threatening step forward. "I'll have none of your lord-of-the-manor charity. You and I are even now. You saved me from prison—or worse. And I've told her"—he nodded toward Andrea, who had been feeling forgotten or possibly invisible—"the truth of the matter."

"And you consider that a fair exchange? Well, who knows. Perhaps you're right," Blakeney said. "But put your stiff-necked pride in your pocket for once, man. We both agree that you have this, and more, coming. If my grandfather had not considered himself immortal, he would have provided for your family. So don't be a damned fool, Zach. Even in America you'll need more than a pretty face to get yourself started." He thrust a packet forward.

Zach Cannon hesitated a moment, then reached out for it. "A loan then," he muttered.

"If that pleases you, a loan it is. Well, then, I collect that's that. God speed you, Zach. Do you know," he said, chuckling, "I'm going to miss you. Really good enemies are hard to come by. Here's my hand on it."

Once again there was the merest moment of hesitation, then Zach Cannon grasped the proffered hand. "Well, your lordship"—he twisted the title mockingly on his tongue—"I'll not soon forget you

183

either." And with a nod Andrea's way, "Miss Prior," he was gone.

Lord Blakeney continued to hold his position just inside the doorway while he impaled Andrea with a cool blue stare. She could not force herself to meet his eyes.

"Well?" he said.

"Well what?"

"Isn't there something you'd like to say to me?"

She struggled to find the proper words, then gave it up to evade the real issue between them. "You certainly were generous with Mr. Cannon just now," she substituted.

"Do you really believe so or are you secretly thinking that I gave him an empty packet?"

"I think no such thing," she retorted hotly. "I just said you were generous, did I not? And I could add that I think you and he have the most peculiar relationship I have ever seen."

"Oh, it's not so odd really, considering that my grandfather was his father. Which makes him my— never mind. Zach has always been jealous as the very devil of me for being born on the right side of the blanket. Can't say as I blame him. In his position I'd feel the same. So you see I wasn't so generous after all. Just giving him his due."

"Oh."

"No need to look so shocked. It happens all the time, you know."

"You, I collect, would be an authority on such things."

"Now there you go again. If you're implying that I have a bunch of little woods colts running about the place, I can assure you, you are dead wrong."

"I beg pardon. I should not have said what I did."

"Your apology is accepted. As far as it goes."

For the first time she looked him full in the face. "You really want me to grovel for my mistake, don't you?"

"Dashed right I do."

"I don't see why I should have to—" She broke off suddenly to stare at his coat. "What on earth is that?"

"What is what? Oh, that." He gave his sleeve a careless glance. "Why, I do believe it's a paper heart."

Andrea's real-life organ suddenly plummeted. "You're wearing Lady Deborah's heart on your sleeve?"

He frowned. "Perhaps I'm wrong to take offense over the fact that you're constantly misjudging me. I've begun to believe that I don't know you at all, either. You see, until lately, I never took you for a sapskull."

Andrea moved a few steps closer in order to get a better look at the valentine pinned to the blue superfine. "That's my heart you're wearing!" she exclaimed.

He stared intently at his shoulder this time. His lips moved with silent exaggeration over the syllables. "ANDREA PRIOR. Well, damme, so it is!"

"Where did you get it?"

"Found it."

"What do you mean, found it?"

"Well, in the bottom of Emmy's urn, to be precise. It looked so lonesome there after all the others had been claimed that I sneaked it out to save it for a more propitious time."

"And this is a more propitious time?"

"Well, no, not really. But it seems to be the only time I have, since Emmy tells me you plan to leave tomorrow. So that rather forces me to speed up the wooing. Of course," he said reflectively, "if we count the time I fished the frog out of your bosom, and the two incidents at the cottage, and especially the time you fell asleep in my arms in the churchyard, well, by Jove, I'm farther along in the wooing department than I've given myself credit for." The mischievous smile that had always had the power to both infuriate her and melt her heart lit up his face.

"It's . . . uncivil of you to bring all that up again."

"And," he retorted, "it's uncivil of you not to admit that you misjudged me. Cruelly."

"Well, what could you have expected? You lied to those Bow Street Runners with a perfectly straight face. Oh, you were most convincing, sir."

"Thank you, ma'am." He bowed mockingly. "But it is one thing to convince two perfect strangers that you're an unprincipled scoundrel and quite another to have the woman you're in love with—and with whom you've shared some very intimate moments that she's struggling, quite unsuccessfully, to forget—share in their opinion. By George, Andrea, that hurts."

She was staring at him wordlessly. For the fact that her jaw had dropped suddenly was a decided detriment to speech. She somehow managed to rally just enough to close it, draw a deep breath, and try again. "W-what did you say?"

"I said it hurts. You've wounded me deeply, Andrea."

"No, no. I got that part. Before that, I mean. You said you loved me?"

"That's correct. And don't look so surprised. It must be obvious. Look at the cake I'm making of myself. Why, if anyone had told me that I'd actually appear in public wearing this damned piece of paper on my sleeve, I'd have called him a bedlamite for sure.

"Oh, by the by." He tapped the heart. "Is this sufficient humiliation or do you want me down on one knee as well?"

"All I want from you is for you to say why you're doing this."

"I just did say. Pray pay attention. I love you."

"You're sure you aren't taking pity on me? Just being chivalrous, the way you were with Zach Cannon?"

"Chivalrous!" he exploded. "By gad, Andrea, you are one for extremes. And I don't mind saying that I'd rather you'd go on thinking of me as the biggest scoundrel in Christendom than as a modern-day St. George. Chivalry be damned."

He closed the gap between them in record time and took her in his arms.

After a protracted, delightful, and rather naughty interval, he interrupted his lovemaking and held her at arm's length. "Miss Prior, I collect we can now consider ourselves betrothed. And, by Jupiter, I can hardly wait for the nuptials to take place. Who would ever have believed that underneath that prim snow-maiden exterior there lurked an abandoned wanton?"

"Well, you, for one," she retorted. "But, oh, my heavens! What about Lady Deborah?"

He looked puzzled. "Well, what about her? Think she's a wanton, too?"

"I just remembered. Everyone expects you to marry her."

"Then everyone will be fooled, won't they?" He did consider the problem thoughtfully, however. "It would be a nice touch," he said after a moment's reflection, "if we could find someone for her, wouldn't it? But dashed if I can come up with a candidate. Beau won't do. He and Lady Deborah are in the same pickle. They are both looking to wed fortunes. No, Beau will have to stick with Lucy Sanders. And Nigel, God help him, is hopelessly in love with my cousin Emmy. Squire Sanders is a moneybags, of course. But he, no doubt, will marry Mama, which is fortunate for us, my love.

"No, there doesn't seem to be anyone left over for Lady Deborah, does there? A pity, but there it is." He snapped his fingers. "Oh, but I say! I have the very thing. You will simply have to share your little secret with her."

Andrea looked puzzled. "What are you talking about? I have no secret that I could share."

"Of course you have. You can simply tell her that all she has to do is wait till midnight next Valentine's Eve, then run around the church like a lunatic—how many times? Twelve, was it?—chanting 'I sow hempseed, hempseed I sow.' After all, that's how you ensnared me, isn't it?

"Ow!" His laughter stopped abruptly as he stooped to rub his shin where she had kicked it. "By George, you'll pay for that. Come here, gargoyle."

He pulled her roughly back into his arms. But his chosen method of retribution was sadly ineffectual. The penalty clearly did not fit the crime. In fact, it spoke more of pleasure than of punishment.